When He Turned Away, Jenna Caught His Arm.

"What would this…this 'marriage'…entail, exactly?" she asked.

Even through his jacket sleeve, the evocative warmth burrowed into his flesh, causing his skin to tighten and heat. Angling back, he studied her eyes and saw the same charged awareness he felt.

"Being seen together. Buying a ring. Setting a date. Then, when you have the child, we can go our separate ways."

"Do you really believe we can convince people that our engagement is real?"

"Absolutely."

Her eyebrows lifted. "Because in business you're used to bluffing…?"

No, he thought. *Because ever since I laid eyes on you again, all I can think about is taking you in my arms and kissing you senseless….*

Dear Reader,

How lonely our lives would be without love...the unconditional love of a mother, the support and laughter of a sister or dear friend, the passion and commitment of a life partner—a true soul mate. Sometimes love isn't so easy to find. For a lucky few, however, love seems to land in their laps—at the most unlikely time, with the most unlikely person. All at once the sky looks brighter and the flowers smell sweeter.

But what if, after finding the one who makes us whole, we lose him again? How much worse is it if he leaves without a word of explanation? That kind of pain is said to heal over time. Does it?

Twelve years ago, the young man Jenna Darley adored disappeared without so much as a note goodbye. When Gage Cameron returns, now incredibly successful and offering to help Jenna fight for custody of her niece after a family tragedy, she's ready to tell him where to get off. But Jenna comes to discover that true love can survive the toughest of tests. Gage has an even more remarkable lesson to learn—and it begins with trusting himself enough to let go of secrets that could hurt Jenna even more.

I hope you enjoy *Baby Bequest*.

Best wishes,

Robyn

BABY
BEQUEST

ROBYN GRADY

Silhouette®

Desire

Published by Silhouette Books

America's Publisher of Contemporary Romance

SILHOUETTE BOOKS

ISBN-13: 978-0-373-76908-7
ISBN-10:   0-373-76908-3

BABY BEQUEST

Copyright © 2008 by Robyn Grady

Visit Silhouette Books at www.eHarlequin.com

Printed in U.S.A.

Books by Robyn Grady

Silhouette Desire

The Magnate's Marriage Demand #1842
For Blackmail...or Pleasure #1860
Baby Bequest #1908

ROBYN GRADY

left a fifteen-year career in television production knowing that the time was right to pursue her dream of writing romance. She adores cats, clever movies and spending time with her wonderful husband and their three precious daughters. Living on Australia's glorious Sunshine Coast, her perfect day includes a beach, a book and no laundry when she gets home.

Robyn loves to hear from readers. You can contact her at www.robyngrady.com.

With thanks to Tony Mansueto
for his expert advice on helicopters.

Melissa Jeglinski, Jennifer Schober and Shana Smith—
thank you all for helping make *Baby Bequest* my favorite.

One

"If you're here about my father, you're too late." Jenna Darley took time enough to bite back tears and lift her chin. "I buried him two days ago."

Gage Cameron glanced over from where he was crouching on the lawn, introducing himself to the Darleys' curious Alsatian. A moment after his ice-gray gaze found hers, his square jaw relaxed with a smile that was supportive and, in spite of it all, faintly seductive.

Unbidden heat curled low in Jenna's stomach.

Suits worth thousands had replaced the bad-boy jeans he'd worn twelve years ago, but clearly the lone wolf she'd once loved hadn't vanished completely. Good thing she'd made the choice to grow up. Move on.

Too bad he'd done it first.

With a final ruffle of Shadow's ears, Gage pushed to his feet. Taller than she remembered, he brushed his large tanned hands and surveyed the extensive manicured grounds of her family's Sydney home. Not that it belonged to "family" anymore.

Her father, twin sister and brother-in-law were all dead, victims of a freak helicopter crash. Although she'd received the news ten days ago, Jenna still had trouble believing it. Half the time she was crying, or close to it; the other half she felt...*numb*. The horror was real, yet it wasn't.

Earlier this week, while she'd sat, dazed, in a lawyer's office, she'd discovered that her father's entire estate had been left to her stepmother, a polished middle-aged woman whom everyone adored...everyone but black sheep Jenna.

The nightmare didn't end there.

Gage sauntered over, the broad ledge of his shoulders moving in a languid, almost predatory roll. When he stopped an arm's length away, his head tilted and chin tipped lower as if she were somehow broken and he could spare the time to fix her.

"I was tied up in Dubai when I heard," he said in a rumbling voice that had deepened over the years. "I flew back as soon as I could."

Jenna twined her arms over her ribs and pressed the sick, empty ache in her stomach. "A waste of your time, I'm afraid."

Jump on your private jet and fly back to your high-powered lair, she thought. *There's nothing for you here.*

His gaze sharpened as if he'd read her mind. Still he persisted. "If there's anything I can do..."

Her bland expression held. "Thank you. No."

Nowadays Gage raked in millions the way other men raked up leaves. Although his base was Melbourne, Australia, his soaring success was praised in every medium all over the world. From Paris to Penang, wherever Jenna traveled for her freelance writing, Gage's rugged good looks, those piercing gray eyes, seemed to find her—today in the unforgettable flesh.

Unfortunately nothing, including status and wealth, could bring back three members of her family she missed so deeply that she couldn't see this darkness ever lifting. But there was a fourth and final member—her three-month-old niece. It was little Meg that she must concentrate on now.

Anchoring his weight, Gage slid both hands into his trouser pockets. "I'm staying in Sydney for a few weeks."

Through bleary eyes, Jenna tried to focus. "You have business to conduct?" *A few more million to make?*

Raw magnetism radiated from his tall and impressive frame while little other than cool detachment shone from the depths of those crystal-cut eyes. So commanding and assured. She could only imagine how ruthless he'd become.

"Your father would want me to make sure you're all right," he replied.

Her mask broke.

"You were the housekeeper's son, Gage. My father gave you a bed, an education, and you left without so much as a goodbye. I'm sorry, but why do you think he would care *what* you said or did now?"

His eyes narrowed so slightly, so briefly, she wondered if she'd imagined it.

"If I thought it would make a difference," he said, "I'd tell you."

She pinned him with a jaded look then turned and sank onto the wooden slats of a nearby garden bench. "Whatever."

If that sounded dismissive or rude, she simply couldn't help it. What little energy she had left needed to be spent on one thing and one thing only.

Meg.

Guardianship.

What do I do now?

She was that little girl's blood, not Leeann Darley. It was wrong that her stepmother should raise Meg, no matter what that stony-faced lawyer or those wills had said. True, these last ten years she'd had no fixed address, and at present she had no legal right to Meg.

She also had no intention of giving up.

Elbows on knees, Jenna gnawed around a thumbnail. When her restless gaze landed on a stick, she picked it up and tossed it for Shadow to fetch while Gage slowly circled her.

"You and your father always locked horns," he said after a long, considering moment. "Everything was left to his wife, wasn't it?"

A withering, dizzy sensation ran through her. *Everything* was right.

But then she studied him more closely. "What was that? A good guess?"

His mouth tilted. "Surely you've heard of my sixth sense where finances are concerned."

She thought it through and had to concede. Of course Gage's intuition with regard to money matters was well known. Aside from that, it wasn't unusual for a husband to leave the majority of his worldly goods to his wife, including the family property and everything in it.

A dry eucalyptus leaf dropped into her lap. Jenna covered the leaf in her hand and broke it in her fist. The trees had been saplings when they'd first moved here. It seemed that as they'd grown taller, she'd grown more unhappy until one day she'd simply up and left. The frustration of trying to fit in with a blended family…the deep sense of loss whenever she thought of her mother… What she wouldn't give to turn back time to when they really *had* been a family.

But fairy tales were for children. And sometimes even children missed out.

"I don't care about my father's possessions," she said. There were things far more important than money.

"Tell me, Jenna, twelve years on, what *do* you care about?"

She gazed up into that strongly hewn face, at the faint scar nicking his upper lip. "If I thought it would make a difference," she quipped, "I'd tell you."

A lazy grin reflected in his eyes. "Try me."

God help her, she was tempted.

She was light on friends—hopping from country to country didn't nurture long-term anything—and she did have an overwhelming urge to confess to someone who knew her background that she'd forgiven her father for remarrying so soon after her mother's death. It hurt like hell that she'd lost the chance to tell him that she loved him, despite their ongoing feud.

Worse, she would never talk to her sister again, the one person she'd truly trusted. Amy had been more than a sibling, more than a friend. She'd been a *part* of her. And an important part of her sister lived still.

The inescapable truth spilled out. "I have to fight for her child."

His eyebrows nudged together and his hands emerged from his pockets. "What did you say?"

Jenna bit the inside of her cheek, but she couldn't take it back, just as she couldn't will away the salty trail curling around her chin.

She knocked the tear aside. "These last few days have been…difficult."

His frown deepened. "What are you talking about? Whose child?"

"Amy has—" She swallowed against the wad of cotton clogging her throat and rephrased. "Amy *had* a three-month-old."

He sank down beside her, too close and yet, in other unwelcome ways, not close enough. "He didn't mention a baby."

Jenna's attention caught and she looked at him. "Who didn't mention a baby?"

His preoccupied gaze blinked back from some distant point. "I mean the newspaper report my second-in-charge passed on. It only cited your father's widow, yourself and the three passengers who'd flown out to survey a development site."

She nodded as the details looped their well-worn groove in her brain. "Brad, Amy's husband, wanted Dad's opinion on some acreage he was interested in buying. They left at ten in the morning. Meg stayed with my stepmother."

Jenna had originally booked a flight for her niece's christening next month and had planned on staying a while. Amy had been so excited. The sisters saw each other regularly, but as Jenna had grown older—particularly now that she was an aunt—it hadn't seemed nearly enough. But when she'd received news of the accident, she'd boarded the first flight to Sydney.

Before arriving last week, she'd seen photos of her niece. Since the accident, she gazed at them constantly. Her favorite was Meg's first bright-eyed smile, hugging the panda bear her auntie had sent by Express Mail the day Margaret Jane had been born.

Now that little girl had lost both her parents and was living with a woman who cared more about facials and status symbols than lullabies and kisses good-night. At the funeral, Leeann had mentioned that she and Meg would be flying to San Francisco to visit her aging parents for Christmas; she wasn't certain when they'd return.

Christmas was only three months away.

Jenna clutched the bench slats at her sides and prayed.

I'll do anything, give anything. Just help me find a way.

Shadow trotted back and carefully placed the stick at Gage's polished shoes. He stooped, cast the stick spinning with absentminded skill, then laid an arm along the back of the bench. The heat of his hand radiated near her nape and some crazy, needy part of her almost leant back to absorb it.

"Who has the baby now? Leeann?"

She nodded then forced her mouth to work. "She's always wanted a child of her own."

Leeann's parents had shuffled her off to boarding school at a young age. Jenna and Amy had decided that because Leeann hadn't felt loved growing up, there was a great gaping hole where her heart ought to be, and Leeann thought a child would fill it. A couple of years back, in her early forties, Leeann had faced the fact she might never conceive—which couldn't be a bad thing. From what Jenna had sampled of Leeann's parenting skills, a starving rat would treat its young better.

"Amy told me that Leeann was getting desperate," Jenna continued. "She'd looked into in vitro fertilization and even adoption."

After doing a story on an orphanage in the Jiangxi Province last year, Jenna had wanted to adopt every dewy-eyed child there…so vulnerable and innocent. Now there was another orphan in the world.

"She's the testamentary guardian?"

Jenna's burning gaze drifted up from her sandals. "My father and Leeann were both named as Meg's guardians in her parents' wills."

"Not you?"

"I guess Amy and Brad thought if they'd ever needed someone to step in, my father was settled here, while I wasn't in one place long enough to take care of the day-to-day needs of a child."

"They were right." When she slid him a look, Gage shrugged. "I've seen your byline on travel articles from all over the world. The ones I've read were very good."

The compliment sank in. Perhaps she should thank him, but she didn't want flattery. What she needed now was a solution.

"Brad had no living relatives," she continued, peering past the pines to the orchid hothouse her father had loved. "I know they both trusted Dad, and Amy wasn't the type to hold grudges, not even against Leeann." Family fractures had been Jenna's specialty. "But Amy would never have meant for Leeann to take sole responsibility for Meg. No one could've foreseen this kind of tragedy—all three gone. If she had, Amy would have known I'd give up *everything*—" Her rush of words ran dry. "You wouldn't understand."

"Because I didn't have a family I was close to?"

Although he'd crushed her heart when he'd left, she scanned his questioning gaze now and found she didn't want to hurt him. But the truth was too obvious. She pressed her lips together and nodded.

He broke their gaze, threw the stick, and Shadow sped off again. "Have you spoken to a lawyer?"

"My father's. He said babies are a full-time job, and Leeann has the resources and sense of commitment Meg needs. But he's being narrow-minded. There's no reason I couldn't find work here and settle down."

"Would you want to?"

Images of Hawaii at sunset and the iridescent greens of Germany in spring clicked like snapshots through her mind, but she pushed them aside. There was no question. She would give it all up tomorrow.

But if Gage had implied that people who moved around somehow lacked a sense of responsibility… "I doubt you're in a position to cast any stones," she replied.

He flicked open his jacket button and his deep chest expanded beneath his crisp white shirt as he leant back more. "Oh, I understand a wandering spirit, Jenna. Owning stock in companies across the globe gives me a reason to migrate regularly and often. I don't like to grow roots." His approving gaze brushed her cheek. "Neither do you."

A tingling rush swept over her skin, but she wouldn't respond based on physical awareness. Instead she fell back on cynical amusement. "Well, who'd have guessed? We're practically a match made in heaven."

"Heaven's a little too tame for us."

When his eyes crinkled at the corners, a delicious warmth seeped through her veins.

So, after all this time, at their deepest level, they knew each other still. She felt so fragile—so much in need of his strength—she could almost forget the heartache of that summer, fall into those powerful arms and actually forgive him.

A phone rang. Gage slipped the cell from his belt and checked the display. "Excuse me. I'll be five minutes. Ten tops."

Letting go of the tension, she inhaled a lungful of pine air and Gage's frighteningly familiar scent. Then she stood and moved away, leaving Gage to his call.

Her laptop and Internet connection were still open in her father's study. She'd been about to hit SEND and decline an offer on a story about a chain of bed-and-breakfasts from Tuscany down through to Campania when Shadow had barked and she'd crossed to the French doors. A tall dark stranger had been walking up the path from the arched iron gates. Two disbelieving seconds later she'd realized her visitor was none other than the man she'd fallen in puppy love with after her first year of college.

Jenna passed through those French doors now, crossed the spacious room decorated in forest-green leather and handcrafted oak, then folded herself into the chair set before her laptop. Her gaze settled on the photo her father had kept on his desk—herself and Amy, aged eight, in Cinderella dress-up. Amy, the nurturing one, was fixing Jenna's lopsided tiara.

Jenna picked up the photo, as she'd done so often these past days. But this time her thoughts drifted back to her visitor.

Gage and his mother had lived in a house next door, which had been supplied by her father. For five years she'd glimpsed her young male neighbor only at a distance. Then she'd come home from college that summer and the brooding ruffian had grown into a man—deep-chested, muscled and sexy in a dangerous way that had left her breathless whenever he'd looked at her with a slanted smile that said he'd noticed her too.

Puppy love. The term was too naive for the wonderfully wicked feelings he'd planted and nurtured within her. Far more explicit phrases came to mind.

The simmer of remembered longing trickled through her bloodstream then swirled and sparked like a lit match down below. But she shrugged off the smoldering sensation. Her father had said Gage wasn't the type of man a young woman should get involved with.

Jenna rested her forearms on the desk.

Twenty-nine wasn't so young.

"I managed to end that call sooner than I'd thought."

Jenna jumped at the deep voice at her back. She swung around and felt her heart beat faster. Gage's striking silhouette consumed the doorway, eclipsing a good portion of the golden afternoon light.

How many lovers had he had in twelve years? How many times had she secretly wished she'd sampled him herself?

As he moved forward, she tamped down that thought and, after replacing the photo, eased out of her chair.

She searched for something to say. "So, another business deal in the bag?"

"Afraid not. And I won't lay more chips on that table just yet." He flicked back his jacket, set his hands low on his hips and took in the room—the wood-paneled walls, the limestone fireplace, the wingchair where she'd once curled up on her father's lap while he read his botany books and explained the pictures.

"So was Leeann bequeathed the house as well?"

Jenna slid her attention from the chair back to Gage and gave him a wry smile. "Leeann's been generous enough to let me stay while I'm here. She and Meg are in the penthouse in town."

"Do you have savings? I presume you won't starve."

She might not be wealthy by his standards, but who was? "I haven't lived off my father since I left college and found my first freelance job overseas."

He came closer and her center warmed as that lit match flickered and leapt high. It wasn't the place— certainly not the time—and yet the burning physical response to his being near was automatic, a literal knee-jerk reaction. Did he have that effect on all women? The answer was obvious: *no question about it.*

"You really don't care about the business, the house?" he asked, a curious light in his eyes.

That inner warmth wavered and fell away.

"My family, bar one, are gone. No, Gage, I don't care about the money."

Landing back in reality, all the pain fresh again in her mind, she crossed to the door. For more reasons than one, it was time to end this reunion.

"Thank you for making the trip. If you don't mind, I think it's best you leave now."

Deep in thought—also ignoring her suggestion—he moved to the desk. "I'll speak with my lawyer."

Over a decade on and *still* he didn't listen. "I just told you—"

"Not about the money. About your niece."

She shut her eyes and groaned. "Please don't."

The last thing she needed was a Family Court judge bristling over the heavy-handed tactics of a multi-millionaire who thought he could buy anyone and anything.

He eased a thigh over one corner of the desk and laced his hands between his long, clearly muscular legs. One dark eyebrow flexed. "What if it means getting custody of your niece?"

"Gage, please. This isn't a game."

But the steely look in his eyes said he was very serious.

He picked up a miniature globe and spun the sphere. Asia, Europe, America flew round in a blur of bright colors. "I must say, I'm not wholly convinced you'll be happy giving up your lifestyle. God knows, I wouldn't be."

Self-righteous heat scorched her cheeks. "No problem for you." Her smile was thin. "Stay single."

His lips twitched as if she'd said something amusing. "I don't see marriage as an issue, necessarily." He set the globe down. "But children need a stable home life."

"Then I suggest you be extra careful about contraception."

The air between them condensed and crackled before he grinned and assured her, "Always."

His hip slid off the desk and he drew up to his full intimidating height while Jenna remembered his mother—wiry hair, vacant expression, a vague smell of whiskey whenever she spoke. If Gage didn't want the responsibility of having a family, she shouldn't be surprised. He'd been sorely deprived of role models. Jenna's own reasons for remaining single were something else entirely.

"We were talking about your niece," he said in a meaningful tone. "I have a way to get you what you want."

His cool eyes sparkled and she was reminded again of the lawless rebel she'd once known. Then, as now, he'd rippled with the promise of a thousand possibilities. At seventeen, almost eighteen, she'd been entranced by it.

Feeling that same tug, she leant further back against the doorjamb. "Just so we're on the same page, kidnapping's not an option."

He didn't crack a smile. "What I propose isn't completely honest, but it's far from a federal offence."

Now she was intrigued.

Weighing the pros and cons, she searched his eyes and finally murmured, "I'm listening."

"Wherever possible, judges like to comply with last wishes. But you *are* this baby's blood relative."

Her shoulders sagged. She'd been through all that. "Dad's lawyer said that's not enough. And the longer Meg stays with Leeann, the less likely the courts will be to uproot her."

"But if you had a suitable place of your own, as well as the legal brains and money to push forward and make an immediate request…"

She frowned. Waited.

"And…"

"You need a secret weapon," Gage said, "that will shoot you ahead in the guardianship stakes."

"A miracle?"

The scar on his top lip curved up. "A husband."

Two

"You're suggesting I get married?" Jenna's hand went to her forehead and she coughed out a laugh, a baffled sound. "I'm sorry. This is taking a moment to absorb but…what would my marrying accomplish?"

Gage's gaze skimmed her shoulder-length dark-blond hair. The soft curl was pretty, but he preferred her hair long, framing a face he'd remembered as saucy, not tearstained.

"For a start," he explained, "a marriage license would tell the court that you're serious about settling down. It would also imply that the child would enjoy the benefits of having a father."

He'd often wondered how different his life might have been had he known positive paternal guidance. Chances were he wouldn't be absurdly rich. Then again, he wouldn't have needed money as a substitute for other, less definable things. Things he'd once wanted to give Jenna but knew now he could never provide.

"Isn't that rather drastic?" she asked.

Gage inhaled her perfume, a scent that reminded him of crushed berries—wild and sweet—then he cocked his head. "I thought these were drastic times."

He looked at her expectantly, but her troubled gaze held far more suspicion than hope.

Hell's fire, the last thing he wanted was Jenna's distrust, even if he well understood it. Twelve years ago he'd vanished like a thief in the night. The time for excuses was long past. But he'd come here today with a plan to help make it up to her. Oh, not entirely—not even close. But maybe, hopefully, enough.

He had it on good authority that Darley Realty, the residential development company her father had founded twenty-five years ago, was in dire financial straits. Gage also knew that Jenna's father had intended to change his will; in the event of his death, the vast majority of Raphael's assets were to pass on to his daughters, not his wife. With Amy gone now, too, Gage had assumed Jenna would be the major beneficiary.

He'd come today to offer to buy Darley Realty for a generous price. He'd wanted a speedy transaction, the idea being Jenna could continue her hassle-free life without learning about the company's problems and consequently suffering any unnecessary sense of embarrassment or gratitude over his offer. He'd had little doubt that Jenna would accept; her profession was writing, and her life was overseas. But apparently Raphael hadn't had time to change his will before the accident. And it seemed that Jenna couldn't care less about the money. After her loss, she had her heart set on one thing and one thing only.

A baby.

Not easy given the circumstances, but he'd learned that almost anything was possible. He'd make it his mission: before he walked away a second time, he would see Jenna happy. He would give her what she wanted most. Then maybe he could close that book—bury that ghost—and at last get on with his life, conscience clear.

She edged toward the middle of the room, hands clasped at her waist. "Say you're right. Where am I supposed to find this husband?"

He tipped an imaginary hat. "At your service."

She smiled. "Now you *are* playing games."

His earlier years had been about survival, pretending offhanded acceptance when mostly he'd been drowning with weights tied around both feet. These days he called the shots. With every breath, he intended to keep it that way. If Gage Cameron played games, it was only ever by his own rules.

"Will you at least listen to my plan?"

"Fine." She nodded. "Go ahead."

"First we'll make it known to Leeann that we're reunited lovers."

Her slim nostrils flared. "First lie."

Not through any lack of desire on his part. But success was bred through a combination of flexibility, critical timing and restraint of emotion. Now he was a master. Now he always won.

"We'll announce our engagement," he went on. "As soon as possible, we'll marry and file a petition for guardianship of Meg. The judge will see that the baby won't need to worry financially—"

"Meg wouldn't need to worry about money with Leeann as a guardian either."

"You said you'd listen," he chided.

Given the way her fingers wound around and strangled each other, she might want to slap him for suggesting any part of this. Instead she nodded again and he strolled toward her.

"Our petition," he continued, "will state that you're not only a blood relative but are also the mother's twin sister. We'll dig up an expert or two who will testify that you're the natural choice to replace the child's biological mother. They can list the benefits the baby would enjoy with regard to face as well as scent recognition. As identical twins, yours and Amy's would be similar."

Her mouth dropped open. "How on earth do you know about such things?"

"I read it somewhere." Since he'd known Jenna, the subject of twins had fascinated him. He'd be happy to recite some eye-opening facts he'd mentally filed away regarding studies on twin science; he bet she'd be interested. "Another advantage is age. You're fifteen years younger than Leeann."

Her eyebrows knitted. "That sounds like discrimination."

"Statistics will bear out the probability that you'll be around longer, which equates to more stability for Meg."

"More stability," she murmured, understanding. "I see."

"Plus you'll have the unswerving support of a marital partner...a past associate of the family."

Her eyes glistened, probing his as she soaked it all in. She'd become far more beautiful than he'd ever imagined. In her female prime, she was lush and challenging, unlike the first time when she'd been young, eager and way off-limits. Her father had been right about one thing: his young blood had run hotter, faster, back then. If he hadn't left that night…

"Why are you doing this?" she asked.

He willed his gaze to track up from the beating hollow of her throat. "You want your niece."

"I could tell the greengrocer that. He's not going to propose."

How to explain?

He tugged an earlobe. "Your father…"

"My father would roll over in his grave at the thought of us marrying. You know that as well as I do."

The knife twisted in his gut but he didn't flinch. A poker face was a strategist's best friend. "When we first knew each other, no doubt. But money changes a lot of things, including people's opinions."

"It doesn't change the past."

He knew the questions that shone from the depths of her eyes: *Why did you leave? Why didn't you have the decency to tell me?*

Would she believe that he'd had no choice? Twelve years ago, for the first time in his life, he'd made the smart choice instead of the rogue one. As a consequence, he'd discovered who he was—who and where he needed to be. Free, alone and reasonably happy. He was wise enough now not to wish for more.

He edged around her unspoken question. "If I'd said goodbye, I wouldn't have wanted to go."

God knows, that was true.

Her lips hardened to a flat line. "Here's a cliché that works. I was young and foolish. I thought you cared.

It might be even more foolish to believe that you care to this extent now."

"You think I'd offer something like this then walk away?"

Her eyes held his. "Yes, I do."

"I give you my word."

"Honor was never your strong suit."

But she was forgetting…once when he could have taken her, a virgin, he'd left her alone. Hell, his mother had come from a nice family too until his father had ripped it out from under her and left her with an addiction as well as an infant she couldn't care for.

He inhaled deeply.

All that was done with, buried. Dead. Obviously so was this discussion.

"Then I take it your mind is made up," he stated with a smile that held no offence. When all was said and done, there wasn't a reason in the world she *should* trust him. Regrettably it seemed too much had happened and too much time had passed to change that now.

"My deepest condolences on your loss," he said, "and best of luck with your niece."

But when he turned away, she caught his arm. Even through his jacket sleeve, the evocative warmth burrowed into his flesh, causing his skin to tighten and heat. Angling back, he studied her red-rimmed eyes and saw the same charged awareness that he felt, as well as thinly veiled fear.

Her throat bobbed on a swallow. "I'm just not certain this is the way."

"What other way is there? You've already said that kidnapping's out."

It took a moment for her to return his crooked smile.

But he didn't miss the fine sheen erupting on her hairline.

Finally she blew out a breath and her hold on his arm slid away. "What would this…*marriage* entail?"

He faced her full on. "Being seen together. Buying a ring. Setting a date."

"What about your work?" Her eyes dulled with skepticism. "Do you have time for this kind of charade?"

"I do have several important business transactions coming up, but, as I said, I'll be in Sydney for a few weeks. I'll try to limit my travel after that to keep the pretence up. And once you have guardianship of the child, and there's no chance of things unraveling, we can go our separate ways."

She rubbed her palms down the sides of her jeans. "Do you actually believe we can convince people that our engagement is real?"

"Absolutely."

Her eyebrows lifted. "Because in business you're used to bluffing?"

Because since I laid eyes on you again, all I can think about is taking you in my arms and kissing you sense-less.

His thoughts might have shown on his face since she blinked several times and a blush crept from her cleavage all the way up the column of her throat.

He rapped his knuckles against his thigh and crossed back to the desk.

One step at a time.

"We'll need to show the world," he explained, "that we've fallen in love. That we're committed to each other."

He collected a silver framed photo next to the globe and clenched his jaw.

What a waste. Amy had been a nice girl; *too* nice for his tastes. It had always been Jenna who'd caught his interest, the teenager with a wiggle in her walk and a sense of right on her side. Once upon a time he'd honestly hoped they would marry. If only things had been different…

He pushed *if onlys* from his mind, set the frame down, and met Jenna's gaze again.

She seemed to be sizing him up. "And what precisely do you get out of all this?"

He merely smiled. "I get to help an old friend."

"That's not a very good answer."

"It's the only answer I have."

"You mean it's the only one you're prepared to give. Forgive me if I'm a little skeptical of your motives."

"What other motives could there be?"

She pressed her lips together as if they'd gone dry. "You wouldn't expect us to…I mean…you're not thinking that…"

An adrenaline surge threw his heartbeat into a cantor. "You're asking if we'll need to embrace…to kiss?"

Make love?

He crossed back and invaded her personal space until her neck arced slowly back. Gazing down into her eyes, he enjoyed a deep stir of desire—the same as long ago, yet somehow deliciously different.

"Jenna, we need to get something out in the open. Two people know when they're sexually compatible. We were compatible then. We still are now. It would be crazy to deny it. And, yes, we will need to show affection in public. But I won't take advantage of the situation."

Naturally he wanted her, but that could only happen if she wanted him, too. And not out of comfort from grieving, or impossible dreams of *happy families,* but from a mutual hunger that deserved to be satisfied, once…possibly twice. That was the limit. That would be safe.

Calm, mingled with curiosity, washed over her face. "You're a complicated man, Gage Cameron."

"That's where people come unstuck." He grinned. "I'm easy to work out."

He imagined his palm sliding down over her curves, his head lowering and insides smoldering as his mouth captured hers. She was frightened, filled with pain and a desperate need for reassurance. How easy it would be to meet her lips and give her some relief.

He bit down and moved away.

Time to go.

"I can get things underway tomorrow," he said, almost to the door. "I'll collect you at ten."

"Gage?"

He turned back.

"I'm not sure I won't regret this, but…" She hesitated then slowly smiled. "Thank you."

He nodded and left, the dog trotting at his heels.

When Jenna had what she needed—when there was no question—he would walk away, just as he was walking away now. Because her father had been right. Long term he was bad for her.

Hell, too close for too long, he was bad for anyone.

Three

The next day Jenna accepted Gage's hand and let him help her out from his black imported coupe onto the sidewalk that surrounded her stepmother's apartment building. Peering up at the top floor, she sucked in a nervous breath and straightened her conservative, pale blue dress.

She hated conservative. A T-shirt and jeans suited her far better. But denim would look decidedly out of place today alongside Gage's craftsman-cut suit. Not that his long, powerful legs wouldn't still look exceptional in faded hip-riding Levi's. Whenever she'd seen him during that summer long ago, hunched over the open bonnet of his eighties model Ford—his broad, bare back glistening and brown—she'd practically melted.

"We don't need to do this today." He placed a warm

palm between her shoulder blades. "You can give yourself another day or two."

His words, and touch, almost melted her now. And after yesterday, when he'd stood so close and had spoken about *affection in public* and *sexual compatibility*, she was certain any significant physical contact between them would be as dangerous as ever. Yet, for the sake of authenticity leading up to their "marriage," he'd made it clear they needed to play, and play well, at being lovers.

So how soon before he brought her close to him? How soon before they kissed?

"After hearing your lawyer's advice half an hour ago," she said, forcing herself to focus, "seeing Leeann sooner is definitely better than later."

He walked in step beside her. "Lance sounded more than optimistic about our chances."

She clutched her handbag to her chest. Her stomach was a constantly churning ball of nerves. "I'm not sure he bought the reunited lovers story."

She wasn't any more certain Leeann would. Jenna loathed being deceived and hated deceiving anyone else. But as Gage had pointed out, these were desperate times. And the next few weeks weren't to benefit herself but her niece. Despite the guardianship directive, in her heart she knew Amy would have given more than her blessing—she'd have been cheering her on every step of the way.

Gage sent her a lopsided *trust me* smile that made Jenna's heart skip a beat. "My lawyer isn't the one who counts. We need to convince Leeann that we're serious and she's in for one hell of a fight if she doesn't consent to handing Meg over. She'll back down."

Jenna wasn't so sure. "Leeann had three miscarriages early on. I can't see her simply handing over what she wants more than anything." She glared straight ahead. "All the better if she thought it hurt me."

He swung open the building's pedestrian gate and ushered her through. "Leeann can be a possessive and spiteful woman."

Curious, she stepped under the bridge of his arm into the neat sandstone courtyard. "I didn't realize you knew her that well."

"I know enough."

Possessive…spiteful. Could he really help her get custody of Meg from Leeann? Jenna knew where her niece belonged, and not purely because she was kin. She'd never liked or trusted Leeann. Her skin crawled to think of Amy's daughter growing up with a woman who'd reminded her of a prickly, well-dressed praying mantis. She wondered how her father had ever fallen in love with such a woman when her mother had been so sweet and giving—so much like Amy.

They stopped before the building intercom. He gazed down at her, one imperious eyebrow raised. "You ready?"

"No," she replied. "Are you?"

He grinned, slow and sexy. "I'm looking forward to it."

While he buzzed, Jenna wrung her purse and told herself to breathe, just breathe. It didn't help. Would all this subterfuge blow up in her face? Could this hurt her chances with Meg rather than help?

Perhaps she needed more time to think it over.

"Maybe we should have called," she reasoned, "to let her know we were coming."

"No. We should let her enjoy the surprise."

Like the way he'd surprised her yesterday, by showing up unannounced then suggesting they get married? Gage had let her know that he had no intention of finishing what they'd started all those years ago: he didn't plan to seduce her. A big part of her—the pride-filled part—rejoiced. She'd been a fragile teenager when he'd left her love for him high and dry; she hadn't thought she would ever recover.

Yet a more reckless side remembered the feel of his hard, hot chest, the way his shadowed jaw had grazed a delicious path along her skin. What would it be like to enjoy the penetrating pleasure of his kiss again? Would it feel different now that they were older?

The intercom clicked and Leeann's voice purred out. "I'm busy. Come back later."

Gage leant closer. "Mrs. Darley, this is Gage Cameron. I'm with Jenna. May we come up? We won't take more than a few minutes of your time."

A torturous silence stretched out. Jenna imagined her stepmother's mind spinning at the name from the past, connecting it with "multimillionaire" then wondering why the heck he was troubling her almost two weeks after her husband's death.

The intercom snapped again. "I really am stretched for time."

Jenna set her teeth. She was so over Leeann's lady-of-the-house routine. She'd been over it years ago. Today, for her niece's sake, she wouldn't tolerate it.

She spoke directly at the grill. "We've come to see Meg."

Large hands on Jenna's shoulders tugged her back. Gage's slight frown said, *I'll handle this.* "Mrs.

Darley, I'm on a tight schedule, too. We would appreciate a few moments."

Jenna had all but given up when the door buzzed, and her high-strung nerves loosened a knot. Gage shouldered the jamb and swept Jenna inside the building. At the lift, he punched the *up* arrow.

Threading his hands before him, he gazed at the light passing down the floors—so cool—while she felt ready to dissolve like a sandcastle smashed by a succession of waves. But this morning, whenever her mind had funneled down into grief-stricken thoughts over losing her father and sister, she'd ordered herself to think only of Meg. More resolute than ever, she did that now.

Beside her, Gage rocked back on his heels. "Why did you cut your hair?"

His question threw her. She looked over at his classically chiseled profile—the straight nose and firm jaw angled up as he watched the lift light blink down.

"I'm sorry," she stammered, "what did you just say?"

He looked at her, the same way he had yesterday—evaluating, wondering. Dangerous and sultry. "When I left, your hair was a thick wavy river down your back."

What on earth?

Gathering herself, she forced her eyes away from his and dead ahead. "Most places I stay don't have dryers. It was difficult to manage."

"It was beautiful."

The breath caught in her chest. Was he doing this deliberately—putting her off-guard, now of all times? Or was he setting the mood for their performance in front of Leeann? Either explanation made her less than comfortable. In fact, it made her highly *un*comfortable.

She blew a wave off her damp forehead and concentrated on the cold metallic doors. "My hair isn't important."

"I liked when you wore it out, wild and tangled."

"It's much easier tame and shorter."

Out of the corner of her eye, she saw him appraise her, from crown to toe, before he peered back at the lift light. "You should let it grow."

Heat consumed her cheeks. Feeling herself being towed away, Jenna briefly closed her eyes and tried to tamp down images of him curled over her, his hands in her hair—long, short…what did it matter? Making love with Gage would be ecstasy any way it came.

The lift doors whirred open. They stepped inside and traveled to the top floor in simmering silence. The space seemed way too small to accommodate her, him and the electric charge humming between them.

When the lift stopped, she strode out a step ahead then had to tell her heart to quit thumping all over again. Leeann was parked in the doorway of what had been, only a handful of days before, her father's apartment.

Jenna had always disliked the beauty mark that sat on the steeple of Leeann's left eyebrow. She detested it more now as that eyebrow lifted along with her stepmother's intrigued smile.

Leeann spoke to Gage. "Well, *you've* grown up."

"In every way that counts." Gage linked an arm around Jenna's waist and moved them both forward.

Jenna was normally a patient person, but she didn't want to waste time on pleasantries now. As they crossed the threshold onto white Italian marble surrounded by sumptuous furnishings, as politely as she could, she came right to the point.

"Where's Meg?"

After closing the door, Leeann led them into the living room that boasted a panoramic view of the glistening blue harbour and majestic giant shells of Sydney's Opera House. Her father's portrait hung on the far wall and the bonsai plant her mother had given him the year she'd passed away sat on the wet bar. The leaves were tinged brown.

"You should have called and let me know you were coming," Leeann explained, her voice saccharine sweet. "The baby's out, I'm afraid, getting some fresh air with the nanny. She's a woman with impeccable qualifications and references. Expensive, but my granddaughter deserves the best."

"So, you're not caring for Meg yourself?"

Jenna's gaze snapped over to Gage and she smiled. *Good question.*

"Given that I don't have any firsthand experience with infants," Leeann replied a little stiffly, "I wasn't too proud to seek assistance." She brought her hands together, a terminating gesture. "I'd offer you refreshments, but I have an appointment with my lawyer in an hour."

Jenna's lip curled at the same kind of dismissal she'd heard from this woman too often in the past. Then she noticed something out of place—a jacket lying over a dining room chair. A heavy jacket…leather. Big.

She moved toward it, assessed the jacket, then Leeann. "Unless his tastes changed radically, this didn't belong to my father." It smelled of oil or grease.

Leeann stood very still, as if she were holding her breath. "That belongs to the nanny."

"Don't nannies wear pinafores and carry umbrellas?" Jenna asked skeptically.

Leeann manufactured a laugh and patted her blond chignon. "I meant the nanny's boyfriend."

Somebody's boyfriend, Jenna thought, but not the nanny's. Seemed it hadn't taken Leeann long to fill her poor father's shoes.

Her chest constricted.

Or perhaps Leeann had been seeing someone on the side all along.

Leeann swung her attention to Gage. "I presume you made the journey to pay your respects to my husband. A little late for the ceremony, I'm afraid."

Gage nodded. "Jenna's father was very generous to me."

Leeann's green eyes lowered even as they gleamed. "And to me."

A weak mewling leaked out from behind a partly closed bedroom door. Jenna stilled, heard it again, then held her stomach. *Meg.*

A fierce protective instinct surged up and she pushed past Leeann into the room. In the darkened far corner stood a cot, pretty with lace and a hanging mobile of colorful clowns. Tiny fists waved above the mattress and the crying grew louder.

Heart squeezing, Jenna rushed to the cot.

Leaning over the rail, she carefully scooped the baby out and cradled her close. Meg hiccupped out another cry, but her big blue eyes, wet with tears, opened to gaze into Jenna's. Did the baby recognize her? Did Meg think she was her mother?

For the most part, Leeann had made Meg unavailable for one reason or another, although she had been uncommonly generous the day of the funeral; Jenna had held her niece right through the service and afterward at the wake. But that day Jenna had been in a different zone, barely functioning. Now, however, she felt the connection between them as if she'd been zapped by lightning—strong, bright and formidable.

Tucking Meg close, Jenna breathed in the scent of powder and felt the deep-rooted knowledge of kinship. "It's okay, sweetie." As the crying petered out, she smiled softly down as her throat thickened. "You look so much like your mother."

Behind her, she sensed Gage's towering presence, then heard the comforting rumble of his voice near her ear. "And her aunt."

From the rear of the room, Leeann made her excuse. "I'd just put her down and didn't want her disturbed. I wasn't sure you'd understand."

You're right, Jenna thought. *I don't.*

But she kept those comments to herself. Leeann's explanation might be embarrassingly lame, but Jenna didn't want anything upsetting the baby again.

In the absence of a challenge, Leeann went on. "She's sleeping through the night now. Amy used to speak often about what songs Meg liked to hear, the nightlight she preferred left on. Amy might have told you, too, Jenna…over the phone or in a letter." Her voice crept closer. "When did you say you were heading back overseas?"

Jenna curled a finger around Meg's silken cheek. "I'm not."

She smiled at the baby gripping her finger as well

as Leeann's stunned silence. In the past she'd never gotten the upper hand as far as this woman was concerned. That's why she'd left home so soon after finishing college. No matter the disagreement—bar two—her father had sided with his new wife. He'd valued their marriage, as he'd valued Jenna's mother until her death. He'd told his daughter he didn't want any upsets in the family home, then had asked why she couldn't simply be polite and get along.

Her father couldn't understand that Leeann had seen his strong-willed daughter as a threat. When they were alone, Leeann had made it clear there was room for only one mistress in the Darley household. The frosty glares, the subtle yet painful barbs… Having been brought up by a quiet and gentle woman, Jenna hadn't known how to handle a female relationship based on rivalry. In the end, she'd handled it by throwing up her hands and walking away.

But she wouldn't walk away from this fight.

"Wasn't there an assignment," Leeann stammered, "in Italy? You mentioned it at the funeral…"

Gage blocked Leeann's progress toward Jenna. "She declined that assignment. Although we have talked about visiting Venice during a brief honeymoon."

Every inch of Jenna glowed warm. Those words were simply part of an act to get Meg and keep her where she belonged. Yet it seemed like only yesterday that she'd gone to sleep dreaming of sharing a honeymoon with Gage. A young and foolish girl's dream. She had never featured in his bigger plans.

Now Gage was an important man, and pedal-to-the-metal busy.

Why *was* he helping her?

Ashen-faced, Leeann navigated around Gage and planted herself before Jenna. "Did I hear right? A honeymoon?"

Gage cupped Jenna's shoulders and his heat radiated through to her very bones. "When Jenna and I met again, the old sparks fired back up." He looked down at her and smiled. "We've wasted so much time, haven't we, darling?"

His earlier comments about her hair rose in Jenna's mind. Finding the emotion she needed, she bit that bullet. "When Gage asked me to marry him, I…I knew it was right." She turned, steadied herself upon facing the solid heat of Gage's frame, then placed the baby in his arms.

Strong chin tucking in, he held Meg a little away from his broad chest…until the baby gurgled, then he cocked his head, his mouth curved slightly at one corner, and he brought her close.

A tower of a man holding such a tiny life. The picture made Jenna's heart beat fast. Gage had no intention of fathering children. As he'd said, he valued his freedom too much and a child needed stability. Still, it was a shame that a man who possessed Gage's more admirable qualities—leadership, intelligence, vision—would never pass those genes on. This situation with herself and Meg would probably be the closest he would come to fatherhood.

A shiver chased up her spine.

Gage could walk away. But, as young as she was, would Meg grow attached?

Would her Aunt Jenna?

Although Leeann was inches shorter than her stepdaughter, she managed to look down her long nose at her. "I don't see a ring on your finger, Jenna."

Gage directed his smile and attention toward Meg but spoke to Leeann. "That's where we're headed next."

Clearly agitated, Leeann patted her chignon again then moved to pry the baby from Gage's arms. "Then I suppose you'd best be on your way."

The baby squirmed, but Leeann propped Meg upright against her shoulder, facing her away from the couple she was obviously seeing more clearly as a threat. When Meg mewled, Leeann rubbed the back of her pink playsuit a little too vigorously. The truly tragic part was that Jenna knew how genuinely Leeann wanted to keep the baby, too. Leeann thought Meg could fill that empty place inside of her—the part that hadn't received or learned how to love. If Jenna hadn't experienced Leeann's narcissism firsthand growing up, she might even feel sorry for her.

"You'll both be living in Melbourne?" Leeann asked, her eyes assessing the two of them.

Jenna's mind went blank. Now that she was back, she had no intention of leaving Sydney again; this had been Amy's home. It would be Meg's home too. But Leeann would be aware that Gage's headquarters were down south.

As if reading her thoughts, Gage came up with the perfect response. "Jenna would like to stay in Sydney, and I already had plans to relocate my head office here."

His arms circled Jenna's waist and brought her closer. As he smiled down into her eyes, her heartbeat tripped over itself. He was so convincing. She had to remind herself that these simmering looks were merely for show.

Leeann cleared her throat; their display obviously irritated her. "I read in this morning's business section that you were wrapping up a secret negotiation." The baby whimpered and Leeann began to jiggle her. "I'd have thought your time would be needed in Melbourne twenty-four seven."

When the baby cried, Leeann shh'ed louder and jiggled faster, and Jenna's paper-thin patience tore down the middle.

She couldn't do it. Legal guardian or not, how could she leave Amy's baby here even one minute longer?

She was about to lever Meg from Leeann's arms when a young woman rushed into the room.

"I'll take her if you'd like, Mrs. Darley."

The woman's glasses sat crookedly above the bump of her nose, but her bearing, as she held out her hands for the baby, was firm and confident. Although she didn't want to, Jenna took a step back and let the woman—Meg's nanny, she presumed—take her niece.

Behind small oval lenses, the younger woman's large dark eyes appraised her, but Jenna couldn't quite decide whether it was with approval or mistrust.

"You must be Meg's aunt." The nanny smiled down at the quieting baby and tickled her chin. "I can see the resemblance." She turned to Leeann. "I had trouble finding the right formula. I'll make a bottle then put her back to sleep."

Leeann's chest expanded with a shuddering breath as she set a hand to the bodice of her raw silk jacket and visibly composed herself. "Thank you, Tina. We'll leave you both alone. My guests were about to leave."

Gage drew a card from his jacket's top pocket. "My lawyer's number." His grin was cold. "In case you need to contact us."

Traveling down in the lift a moment later, Jenna couldn't stop quaking. She crossed her arms, raised a fist, and tried to find a finger with any nail left to bite. She hadn't chewed her nails since ninth grade when Amy had bought a DIY French tip set to help her quit the habit. Amy had said there was no excuse for biting nails…she had to be strong…had to take it one day at a time…

Tears thickened in her throat.

Meg crying, the nanny's judgmental gaze, Leeann pushing them out… She should have taken her father's bonsai and *smashed* it against the window of that damn million-dollar view! Or better yet, she should have brought it back home where it belonged.

She closed her eyes.

Oh, Meg…

Gage wound an arm around her bent shoulders and brought her close. But the swelling bank of tears only rose higher. He felt so strong and sturdy, a pillar she could lean on. Lord in heaven, she needed that so much.

Releasing a breath, she relented and buried her face against a chest carved from warm granite.

"This is so wrong," she groaned against his lapels. "Meg doesn't belong there."

Gage's large hand stroked her hair.

The sheer strength of him…the smell. How easy it would be to forget the past and believe this incredible man truly wanted to marry her, and not merely for pragmatism's sake.

Her hands curled, fisting in his jacket.

Oh, I really am in a bad way, she thought.

As the doors parted, he gently drew her away and gazed deeply into her eyes, reassuring her. "The nanny seems nice."

Wishing away the hollow ache in her chest, Jenna accepted the handkerchief he offered and dabbed her wet eyes; she could imagine the puffy smudges partially covering her hideous dark circles. God, she needed sleep.

She sniffed. "I guess things could be worse."

But not much.

After she returned the handkerchief, Gage took her hand and, with a determined stride, marched one step ahead out of the lobby and into the street.

Behind his striding size twelves, her heels clacked on the sandstone. "Where are we going?"

"You weren't listening earlier?"

Her mind rewound and a wave of butterflies released in her stomach. "We're going to buy a ring?"

"A diamond so outrageously large that no one, including Leeann, can miss it. Then we have another stop to make."

He swung open the car door and indicated that she should take the passenger seat. She eased in and peered up at him. "Another stop? Are you going to tell me?"

Before shutting her door, he winked. "You know how I like surprises."

Four

Jenna gazed at the glamorous, princess-cut, white diamond ring Gage had slipped on her finger an hour ago and swallowed a great lump of nerves.

"Gage, maybe we're moving too fast."

Sitting across from her at a city mall café, her companion's gaze slid from the waiter delivering his coffee directly onto her.

"You heard my lawyer this morning," he said, a line cut between his brows. "Our best chance of claiming your niece means moving forward now. That translates into getting married immediately."

Jenna propped her pounding head in her hand.

One week, two tops, and I'll be Gage Cameron's bride, she thought. The scenario was surreal. So much had happened lately—the accident, the fallout from the wills, Gage showing up out of the blue. Her poor mind could barely keep up.

Jenna pushed three travel brochures around the tabletop while the diamond sparkled up, dazzling enough to hypnotize.

The Beauty of Bermuda.

New Zealand Honeymoon Retreats.

Marry in Las Vegas!

Time was of the essence, so Gage had suggested countries whose marriage laws required less lead time than Australia's one-month proviso, yet were still recognized here. It made perfect sense. Yet it all felt so…rushed.

Her fingertip trailed down a bright Bermuda beach. The pamphlet featured a couple kissing, their embrace framed by the halo of an orange setting sun. She pictured herself and Gage in that shot and the frazzled knot in her stomach pulled tighter.

"I know this marriage is all for show. I mean, I know this isn't for real." It certainly wasn't for forever.

Although his face was set, the assuring slant of his mouth was still killer sexy. *Darn the man.*

"You shouldn't look at this in terms of a conventional union," he told her.

Jenna sighed. "That's my problem. I'm scared to death no one will see it as conventional. Just phony."

"You're forgetting our chemistry." His gaze rested on her lips, making them tingle, before his attention drifted toward finding his coffee cup and spoon. "If we let that chemistry work for us—"

"Then I could be in even deeper trouble," she muttered under her breath.

He dropped in sugar and stirred. "I don't see how."

Well, she could start with how he'd described her hair when they'd stood outside that lift earlier today…the way his graveled confession of how he preferred it wild and tangled had made her heartbeat race and palms grow damp. He was trouble…trouble with a capital T.

The last thing she needed was to fall in love with Gage Cameron again, particularly when she felt more vulnerable than ever before. She needed to be strong, shore up her defenses, and remember he was here only for the short term. She couldn't handle another dose of heartache—not on top of everything else.

"I don't want this…*relationship* to do more harm than good," she explained. "I don't want it to get out of hand."

"Out of my hands, Jenna, or yours?"

As he sipped his coffee, the power of his lidded gaze seemed to rope around her and tug her in. The awareness glittering in his eyes was so magnetic, so intense, he might as well have thrown a lasso.

She slowly sat back.

Twelve years ago he'd left without a word. Yesterday he'd made it clear he didn't want a family. So, why say in one breath that he wouldn't take advantage of this situation then openly flirt with her the next? He didn't make sense.

Unless…

Gage lowered his cup and scraped back his chair. "We won't waste time arguing the point. If you're unhappy, I'll tell the travel agent to nix the Las Vegas itinerary."

Words sat on the tip of her tongue, but before she could call him back and blurt out heaven knew what, he moved off. Two seconds later, his cell rang.

He'd left the phone on the table when his office had called earlier. He hadn't been pleased at the interruption. In fact, he'd seemed hard-pressed not to hurl the phone at the floor.

Jenna willed the hot-wired tension from her body. Gage was already passing through the travel agency doorway. Whoever it was could leave a message. With Gage gone, she had a little time to mull over her earlier assumption.

Setting her chin in her palm, she fingered the corner of the New Zealand pamphlet.

If it meant getting Meg back, of course she would marry Gage. She was grateful for his help. And if she had to choose, New Zealand's Mt. Ruapehu, with its fairy-tale top-of-the-world chateau, would've been her pick. But from the moment he'd suggested a wedding, a question had sprouted and grown until finally the answer pushed its way into the light.

He'd said he wouldn't take advantage of this situation. That didn't mean he would object if his bone-melting magnetism worked its inevitable charm and she ultimately threw herself at him, either to show her appreciation for his help, or for even more fundamental reasons than that.

Sexual attraction.

Carnal satisfaction.

Gage had found tremendous material success; there were few people to rival his seemingly effortless ascent in the business world. Yet somehow she got the impression that he was secretly looking for a different kind of challenge. Perhaps something over which he'd contemplated as often as she had.

Maybe he did want to help an old friend.

But maybe he also wanted to help himself.

His cell phone beeped, and Jenna's heart leapt to her throat. A message flashed on the miniature screen… and kept flashing. Her gaze snapped over to the travel agency. No Gage yet. When the cell phone beeped again, then beeped louder, an elderly man at the next table frowned at her over his bifocals.

Smiling an apology, Jenna rested her hand over the cell, hoping to muffle the sound. But the buzz vibrated up through her hand; it simply wouldn't be ignored.

More heads turned. Desperate, she swept the phone up. Which button of so many would stop the noise?

About to stab a red key, she froze. A word in the text message caught her attention.

Progress on the Darley bid?

Her world tilted and she almost slid off her chair. Head spinning, she read it again. She held her breath as another message flashed.

Need projection figures for next quarter if proceeding with purchase.

"Anything wrong?"

She tossed the phone as if it were a hot coal. It spun in a wild circle and landed in front of Gage as he joined her again at the table.

Drawing in his chair, he glowered at the phone then at her. "You look as if you'd seen ten ghosts."

"That message…" she managed. "It's about Darley Realty." Trying to make sense of it, her next words squeaked out. "Had you been speaking with my father about his company before the accident? About taking it over?"

The corners of that sensual mouth pulled down as he scanned the message. Then that faint scar twitched.

She heard the rasp of his beard as he rubbed his jaw, then growled and thumbed a button.

Gage, answer me, damn it! "Was Darley Realty the secret takeover Leeann read about in the paper?"

Had she been mistaken about the kind of challenge Gage was chasing? Was taking over her father's company Gage's true secret agenda?

After a strained moment, he loosened his tie and nodded. "Your father was interested in selling."

Jenna expelled a lungful of pent-up air.

Her father had been tight-lipped about his business dealings at the best of times. Given their strained relationship, there was no reason Jenna should have known about a possible sellout. But Leeann might have known. More to the point…

"Why didn't you tell me?" As her pulse thudded in her temples, she narrowed her gaze and tried to decipher the truth behind the pale shadows in his eyes. "Is it because you still want Darley Realty in your portfolio?" Pain stabbed low in her throat. "Were you planning on seeing Leeann about that, too?"

Gage cursed and looked away. "Of course not."

"The thought didn't cross your mind?"

He collected his teaspoon and tapped it against the table. "That's not the point."

"You know, Gage, it really is the point."

A very sharp, potentially ugly point. She needed to know what this was about. These last few days, she'd had more than enough of being set aside.

"You realize that marriage to me and guardianship over Meg won't give you control of my father's firm. Leeann still gets to keep all the assets, no matter who wins custody of Meg."

He swept his spoon away and growled. "You're blowing this out of proportion. Your father's business doesn't even come close to other businesses I control."

"Then why did you want it?"

Heck, maybe his cronies had learned her father's Western Australia property was riddled with gold. Maybe Gage had some twisted megalomaniacal wish to absorb everything that had belonged to the man who'd once offered him charity—food, an education, a roof over his head.

He didn't meet her eyes. "It doesn't matter now."

"Just because you say so?"

His gaze snapped up. "We have more important things to discuss—like guardianship hearings."

She wasn't finished with this hearing yet. Gage had been after her father's business. He couldn't sweep that under the mat. She knew there had to be more to it…something to do with her and Meg.

"I want to know, Gage. I deserve to know."

His cup, almost at his lips, clattered back down, splashing coffee into its saucer. His expression hardened. "Your father…" He seemed to search for words. "He helped me."

Holding her breath, she waited for him to go on and pushed when he didn't. "Helped you? You mean after you left Sydney?"

His voice lowered. "This is complicated."

She crossed her legs and pretended to get comfortable. "I'm sure you've faced worse."

He exhaled and finally nodded. "You remember how we got…close that summer."

Heat scorched her cheeks. She wasn't that naive teenager anymore, the college girl heartsick for the hired help's son, yet the mere thought of how they'd held each other that last time, with the warm air drifting in through the open pool house, sent blood coursing through her veins like molten lava.

She lifted her chin. "I remember."

"Someone else had her heart set on a little clandestine fun, too."

As understanding slowly dawned, her legs uncrossed and her hands gripped the chair. "I don't believe you," she growled. "Amy wasn't even home that summer—"

"Not Amy. *Leeann.*"

Her head kicked back. The sting was so sharp, he might have physically slapped her.

"Leeann made a pass at you?" The idea was so off, so ridiculous, she almost gagged. But then she remembered the way Leeann had looked at Gage today, as if all her lewd Christmases had come at once, and her heart hit the ground.

Dear Lord, it was true. Her father's wife had propositioned the bad boy next door.

She found a thready voice. "What did she say?"

What did she *do?*

"My mother was out. I was in the backyard, working on my car. Leeann called in on the pretence of discussing requirements for a special dinner for some of your father's business associates. She said she wanted to leave a note. I led her to the kitchen, turned back to find a pen…"

When his words trailed off, Jenna finished for him.

"She kissed you."

He rubbed his temple. "I froze, then she snaked her arms around my neck…"

Uneasiness rolled through her, and Jenna waved her hands. "That's enough. I get the picture. But what does that have to do with my father helping you? With you being here now?"

"Leeann's first pass wasn't her last. But I was prepared when she came knocking again. I was inside and didn't let her through the front door. She got annoyed." His bristled jaw shifted. "You know what they say about a woman scorned."

Leeann had known about her crush on Gage, as had her father. Jenna remembered how particularly snide Leeann had been that summer before Gage had vanished and the pieces fell into place.

She'd been jealous.

Gage went on, "Leeann said if I didn't comply she would tell her husband that I'd cornered her in the grounds and forced myself on her."

Jenna's lip curled as she muttered, "And my father loved this woman."

"She kept her word and the next day your father confronted me. Said Leeann had told him everything. I could see in his eyes he didn't believe her. Nevertheless, as her husband, he had no alternative but to act. He told me to pack and be gone within the hour. Along with that, he gave me a good deal of cash and said not to come back unless I could prove my worth."

But Gage hadn't come back…not until yesterday.

"Your mother never knew?" she asked and he shook his head. "She died during my second year of college, didn't she? I was away in Canberra." She'd changed universities, not because of faculty choices, but because she'd wanted to get as far away from home—her unhappy family life and memories of Gage—as she could.

"Your father gave me his word he would look after her," Gage said. "I sent money every month and from my mother's return letters, Raphael kept his word. But it was no secret she was an alcoholic. The addiction took its toll. I came back briefly for the funeral, but Raphael Darley and I only exchanged nods."

She imagined her father's appraising onyx gaze. Had Gage experienced his first business success by then? Had he worn budget trousers to his mother's funeral, or a tailored suit?

She would have come home to pay her respects to Mrs. Cameron—she'd been a kind woman, just so very sad and broken. But her father hadn't told her of Mrs. Cameron's death until some weeks after the event. No doubt he'd wanted to keep the distance between his willful daughter and the young man his wife had accused of attempted rape.

Now Gage had returned home because of three more funerals.

She swallowed the block of wood stuck in her throat. "How long had you been talking with Dad about the possibility of a buyout?"

"We spoke before I flew out to Dubai. Raphael said…" Gage hesitated then continued with more conviction. "He said he was tired and wanted to retire. I said I'd see if I could help."

"And now?"

He leant forward. "Now we have more important things to focus on. Like a white dress and a baby."

His hand rested near hers. When his index finger grazed her pinkie, a jet of nerves and abject longing flooded her system. It was just a touch and yet the anticipation and heavenly heat it caused invaded every cell in her body, making her beat and glow from the inside out.

A white dress…

After a wedding day came the wedding night. He'd said that they would need to put on a show, but was even a portion of her earlier intuition correct? Did Gage have something more than conversation scheduled for behind closed doors?

An image of two bodies, naked and consumed by heightened passion, swam to the forefront of her mind. Fire bloomed in her cheeks, smoldered up her limbs and blew a flame at that private place, low and deep inside.

She set her teeth.

For heaven's sake, think about the baby.

Averting her gaze, she drew her hand away and threaded her fingers in her lap. The diamond twinkled up at her, the embers smoldered again and she looked into Gage's eyes.

"I'm certain we should marry in Australia," she told him in a firm voice. "Leeann will have enough objections and suspicions. We don't need to give her an opportunity to stir trouble over whether a wedding conducted on foreign soil is recognized here, even if it is. It might even delay matters rather than push them forward."

A muscle jumped in Gage's jaw before he shucked back one broad shoulder. "It's your show." He collected his phone. "I'll have my personal assistant track down a good marriage celebrant and make an appointment. We'll get the paperwork filed today."

After thumbing a couple of buttons, he frowned at the screen. "Message from my lawyer." He pressed the phone to his ear. One eyebrow slowly lifted then his face turned dark.

By the time he disconnected, Jenna's heart was pounding in her ears. "What is it?"

Was it about Leeann?

"Your stepmother doesn't waste time," he told her, setting the phone down. "She wants you out of that house. You have a week to find alternate accommodations so Leeann can move back in. And that's not all. She wants to see me two weeks from today at the Darley Realty head office." He grinned. "Let the games begin."

Five

"Welcome to your new home."

As Gage fanned open the door of his three-story penthouse, he fought the impulse to sweep Jenna up, carry her across the threshold and make a beeline for the master suite. Even if he could restrain the urge, the primal messages pulsing through his body didn't lie. He wanted her lines and curves against him. Wanted to hold her, fully, and for the longest time.

This past week had been a blissful kind of torture.

Jenna took a wary step inside and looked around. Curling a wave of hair behind her ear, she took in the extravagantly high ceilings, the king-size crimson-and-cream sunken lounge, then lifted her chin to scan beyond the sheer-curtained glass wall to one of the penthouse's four extensive balconies.

"I really could've found a place of my own. Something slightly less grand than the Taj Mahal," she said, pivoting around. "I'd hate to see your country estate."

He smiled. Maybe one day he'd show her his acreage in Colorado, though he didn't doubt she'd already seen Aspen's spectacular scenery during her travels.

He shut the door and strolled beneath the shadow of a Swarovski crystal chandelier. "We agreed. This is the best-fit solution. Living together is another way for Leeann and her lawyers to understand that we're serious about our relationship."

Her round eyes asked, *How serious?*

He almost stroked her silken cheek as he passed. *Serious enough.*

After visiting her at the Darley address, dining out at casual venues and posing for the press like a regular couple in love, he sensed Jenna was beginning to trust him. No mean feat. He'd hurt her once, but he'd returned to make recompense.

If she decided that she wanted to take this rekindled friendship to the next level—to its delayed but natural conclusion—he wouldn't object. As long as she was fully aware of her actions and his limitations. Whatever they enjoyed, however many times they enjoyed it, it wouldn't be "till death us do part," no matter what papers they signed.

From his first memory he'd wanted to escape—his background, his dead-end life, his sometimes loving, sometimes neglectful mother. When they'd lived alongside the Darleys, Jenna had given him a reason for hope, a reason to stay. Then Leeann had accused him of attempted rape and Raphael had sent him on his way with more money than a regular guy could earn in a year.

The ugly truth was…

At twenty-one, he was relieved to leave "home," and thankful that Jenna had been spared from his less than stellar influence. She'd been way too good for him, a bright young woman from a respectable family. A virgin he had no right to deflower, yet no doubt would have if he'd stayed around for much longer.

As the years rolled on, another truth had bloomed.

No matter how many homes he owned or how powerful he became, the gap between himself and Jenna would never be bridged. He would always feel half-empty inside, missing the ingredient that made other people whole. Whoever's fault that was, it didn't matter. Long story short: his kind shouldn't reach for things they could never hope to have, and shouldn't damage other people when they tried but failed.

Loners shouldn't have families.

If Jenna didn't have her heart set on bringing up her niece…if she didn't want children of her own…well, maybe then. But if he hadn't been good for Jenna back then, he was definitely no good for her now…except where fighting for Meg—her family—was concerned.

An ironic twist, to be sure. But life, he'd learnt, was full of distortions.

"In three weeks," he said, checking the nearby high-tech facsimile for mail, "we'll be Mr. and Mrs. Cameron. Soon after that, you'll gain guardianship of Meg." He turned and offered a teasing grin. "If we're lucky, it might happen even sooner."

While her eyes sparkled with fragile hope, her hands joined, as if in prayer, and pressed against her mouth. "This is about your meeting with Leeann next week, isn't it? You've found something out."

A thread of doubt wove down his spine. But he'd held back these last bits of information long enough. Some she would like, but others…

Regardless, it was time.

"My sources say Leeann wants to sell Darley Realty."

She nodded slowly as if expecting more. "I wasn't sure whether she'd like the idea of being the female figurehead of a successful company like Darley's, or whether it would interfere with her lifestyle. Guess it's the latter. But what's that got to do with our chances of getting Meg?"

He spun a finger in the air. "Rewind a little."

"To what part?"

"The part where Darley's is successful."

Her brow creased. "I don't follow."

"Remember I said your father was tired and wanted to retire? That was only half of it."

Jenna's complexion faded from peaches and cream to the alabaster of the walls in one second flat.

His gut wrenched, but he resisted the urge to comfort her, even while her trembling lips seemed to beg him to do just that.

"Was he sick?" she asked.

He stuffed his hands in his trouser pockets, out of harm's way, and moved forward. "Your father was under a lot of stress. His company had suffered a succession of financial blows, a combination of bad advice and worse luck."

Her face pinched with disbelief. "And he asked you to bail him out?"

He nodded.

Her delicate shoulders, in that simple white T-shirt, stiffened. "I'm still missing a piece, aren't I?"

He hesitated. Should he come clean? Out of necessity, Raphael had told him everything, then had sworn him to secrecy. But Raphael was dead, and Jenna had said it herself: she deserved to know.

He stopped before her and held her eyes with his. "Your father suspected that Leeann was having an affair."

Jenna withered onto the nearby settee as if her legs had dissolved beneath her. She gazed at the floor, her white-knuckled fists clenched at her sides.

"The leather jacket." One fist punched the cushion. "I knew it."

Yes, he'd known it too, particularly given his own experience with Leeann. "I'm not at all sure that your father was still in love with his wife. He was pretty convinced of her infidelity. He wanted to sort out his affairs. Amy's share was already taken care of in his will, although I believe her husband had been wealthy in his own right. But Raphael admitted that he'd written you out after you two had had an argument and you'd left home for good."

He broke off.

Her pallor was much worse.

"You could do with some water," he said. "Or maybe something stronger."

He started toward the black granite wet bar, but she caught his forearm, bare beneath his rolled-up sleeve. The contact was a charge…startling, electric. He inwardly groaned as it shot a white-hot arrow to a highly responsive part of his anatomy.

Tugging, she drew him down to sit beside her. Her voice was a hoarse whisper. "I don't need a drink, Gage. I need to know everything."

The details would hurt but, a week on from their meeting again, he sensed that her strength had returned enough to cope. It had been her personal strength that had initially attracted him to Jenna. Then he'd discovered the power of her smile, the magic of her sigh. How he'd managed to hold off from easing himself fully inside her that last night was nothing short of a miracle.

He took a deep breath.

Stay focused, Cameron.

"Your father was ashamed of writing you out and more ashamed that he'd been too pigheaded to change his will back. He wanted to make amends. He wanted you to come home so he could tell you he was sorry."

As her eyes filled, the muscles in his chest and back tensed. He found her left hand and covered it with his right. That charge again, more intense this time, quickened his pulse to a gallop.

Her glistening eyes questioned his. "But something doesn't fit. If you already knew about the will, why did you pretend to *guess* a week ago that my father had bequeathed everything to Leeann?"

He stroked the top of her wrist with his thumb as he'd done twice before this week—once in his lawyer's office, the second time when they'd visited their marriage celebrant. If the intimacy of that touch was overstepping the line, she'd have let him know. Instead she seemed to take comfort in it. She wasn't the only one.

"The last time we spoke, your father was set to change his will, but he also thought the sale of Darley's might be the sounder option for his purpose of ensuring that his daughters received their inheritance. He wanted to forgive the past and its mistakes and give you, as well as Amy, the proceeds from the sale straight away to save any arguments later. We were going to sign papers when I arrived back from Dubai."

Hanging on each word, she nodded. "But he died before he could change his will or close the deal with you."

"On a business that I still believe will be very profitable when the right measures are in place. Your father…" How to put it? "On top of his suspicions over Leeann, I think he'd simply had enough. I was in a position to help."

"And pay him back for the money he gave you to make your start twelve years ago?"

He shrugged. "It would've been a win-win situation. I get to repay an old debt, attain a company I could build on, and you would've been taken care of." Her hand moved slightly beneath his and that hurtling arrow hit its mark again, the burn hotter and longer-lasting this time.

"I told you before," she said with a reproving but also grateful note, "money isn't important to me."

"But money *is* important to Leeann. She must know now the state of affairs. That there's work ahead if Darley's is to survive. The negotiations were confidential between the two principals, our financial controllers and a couple of my head people. No doubt Darley's man has informed her of the option her husband was looking into."

He sat back against the cream, tasseled cushions. She did too, her lips slightly parted as she listened.

"I'd prefer to win back Meg without this kind of bargaining," he said, remembering the grilling he'd received from Jenna a week ago regarding any plans he may have had to speak with Leeann about a buyout. "But since Leeann has set the agenda, now I'll let her know that I'm willing to pay dearly for the privilege of owning Darley Realty. Then it'll be a question of how dearly Leeann prizes her privileged lifestyle."

"You think she'd exchange Meg for money?" Jenna slipped her hand from his and waved it as she shook her head. "She might not make a cat's mother but she wants a child. You saw how much. She'd have enough funds without your offer. There's the house, the penthouse, Dad's investments—"

"The house is mortgage-free," he said, trying to ignore how much he missed their recent skin-on-skin contact. "But the bank owns the penthouse. The other investments have been converted into funds to buoy a dangerously high overdraft."

He'd been through all the financial details with Raphael. The company was caught in a downward spiral of debt and interest. Only a massive injection of funds could pull it out of the vortex now.

Her jaw was hanging. "Everything gone? Even his holdings in Western Australia?"

"The company still owns that piece of land, but initial reports tell me it's hardly a prime piece of real estate."

"So now we wait and see if Leeann takes the trade?" She winced. "Oh, God, that sounds horrible." Then her back straightened. "But, damn it, I don't care."

He smiled. "That's the spirit." The take-no-prisoners attitude he'd loved so much about her…that was drawing him toward her now, like a line reeling him in.

His groin flexed.

Dear Lord, damming his impulses where she was concerned would never get any easier. In fact, it could only get harder.

Maybe it was time to get things out in the open before he did something he would very much enjoy but quite possibly regret. He'd said he wouldn't take advantage of the situation. It's time he was frank.

Jenna, too.

He threaded his hands and, leaning forward, angled his forearms on his knees. "There's something else we need to discuss about this arrangement. Jenna, we need to discuss us."

A blush crept up her throat and her pupils dilated. She wasn't immune to the heavy-hot strum resonating between them. Clearly she knew what was coming; he merely wanted to know whether to act on it. Was she as curious and flat-out frustrated as he was?

"I need to explain some things about myself," he told her, "and how I feel about you."

Her gaze flared then dropped away to land on the coffee table. She absently collected a pack of cards, which he'd left out this morning, and started to shuffle. "Explain?"

Distracted by the cards, he frowned. "Yes."

"Remember when you explained how to play poker?" She forced a smile as the cards slotted back and forth into her bejeweled left hand. "We stayed up till four one morning. I won."

Frown deepening, he scratched his temple.

From her avoidance tactics, it would appear he'd spoken too soon, if, in fact, there would ever be a right time to speak about the lightning-infused fever that brewed inside him whenever Jenna was near.

Still, he couldn't forget how he'd managed to make her laugh this past week, and how she fit so snugly alongside him whenever they walked. Last night at the movies, when the heroine had walked away from the hero just before the credit roll, Jenna had looked at him. He'd looked at her. Time had sped up and simultaneously slowed to a thick sweetly pitched crawl. He'd come so close to kissing her. He still believed she'd wanted him to.

He sucked down a breath.

He'd been right the first time. They needed this building awareness out in the open. Now.

He reached to take the cards from her hands, but she dodged and shuffled more quickly.

This time, he wasn't put off. "I don't want to discuss poker, Jenna."

Her attention remained on the blur of cards. "You've been playing solitaire, haven't you? That was your favorite. They have that game on software, you know. You can install it on your laptop. You don't need to play the old-fashioned way."

He swept aside a wave curling around her cheek. "I prefer the old-fashioned way."

Her hands stopped moving. Through her white T and fine lacy bra, her nipples visibly tightened. All those years ago, he'd lovingly caressed them. Once, only once, he'd run his tongue around their peaks, grazed his teeth over their ripened swell. Lord have mercy, he could feel their warmth pressed against him now.

"Times have changed." Her voice was uneven, a little breathless. "Don't you think it's only right that we try to change, too?"

This time she let him take the cards and set them on the tabletop. "I don't work that way. How about you?"

Would you like to play, Jenna? The way we used to… Even if it's just once…

He leant forward, inviting her to read the intention in his eyes…to sense how strong that intention was.

Her expression softened, even as her blue eyes grew darker, hotter. Her lips parted and she silently drew down some air. His gaze lingered on her mouth while his surroundings receded and the magnetic field urging them nearer wound up another sizzling degree. He tipped closer, ready to speak.

Ready to kiss…

Two palms met his chest, blocking his advance. "You said you wouldn't take advantage of the situation."

The high-voltage buzz zipping through his veins screeched then fell suddenly quiet. He pulled away, focusing on her words. "If that's what I'm doing— taking advantage of you—I apologize. But, Jenna, we really ought to talk about—"

"You want to *talk?*"

When her lips twitched with skepticism, Gage blinked twice then set his jaw. "After the week we've spent together, the way we've reconnected, I thought you might want to hear what I have to say."

Her gaze flicked over his face. Her expression eased, and for an instant her heart seemed to show in her eyes.

She slowly nodded. "Go on."

He bunched his hands to keep from bringing her near and instead laid an arm behind her over the settee. She didn't move away.

"Like anyone else, I have regrets. I've thought about you, Jenna—about us—a lot over the years."

"It's surprising that you found time to make your fortune."

He saw the flash of regret on her face over the barb, but she didn't take it back.

He conceded. "Guess I deserve that."

"Maybe. I really don't know anymore. I suppose it depends on what you say next."

The strength Gage so admired radiated out, and he caught himself. But he could only be truthful about how he felt. About what he could offer and what he could not.

He wanted to be with her, for her to share his bed, to know each other at last. "I want us to go back and claim what was denied us years ago." By age and class structure, by Leeann and his own shortcomings. "I'm asking if you want to finally live out that experience too."

He paused to find the words that would bind their feelings of the last few days rather than unravel them. He was committed in their efforts regarding Meg; he would be there for her in all things, the very best way he knew how. The thorn in the side of that commitment?

Making love with Jenna and helping her with Meg couldn't transform him into something he was not. He'd been born to be exactly what he was—nothing less, nothing more. For everyone's sake, he needed to remember that.

Against his better judgment, once he'd tried the traditional way. It had ended in the worst kind of disaster.

Rule number one: learn from your mistakes.

He was about to speak when Jenna tipped forward and set her forehead in her hands. Gage shunted closer and his hand lowered from the back of the settee to settle on the warm curve of her back. *Oh, hell.*

"Jenna…?"

She shook her head fiercely. "I can't do this. I want to, God help me, but I can't."

His heartbeat stopped before thudding harder against his ribs. Her words were muffled but he'd heard her well enough.

"I understand now why you left," she went on, "but it still hurt. Gage, it hurt almost as much as anything I've ever had to face."

Anything she'd had to face? Like the accident.

Christ.

Like losing her mother.

His hand came away.

"I can't risk that again," she ground out. "Not when Meg is relying on me. You said it yourself. If we acted on…" She groaned softly and her voice lowered. "On what we're feeling now, it would only complicate matters. The very last thing I want is more complications. I don't need to be hurt again, especially now."

Gage's fist dropped onto the settee with a soft thud.

He'd arrived on his white charger, decked out in shining armor, promising to rescue her. Determined not to hurt her. His goal had been to make her happy. Set things right. Release the ghosts then get on with their lives.

Yet here he was, putting tears back in her eyes. She might still be attracted to him, but she didn't want to take that next critical step. More to the point, she didn't want him to either.

Which meant *hands off.*

Get over it.

Move the hell on.

As she pushed to her feet, her knees in their fashionably tatty jeans bumped the coffee table. The cards, balanced on the timber's edge, fell, spilling over the marble floor.

She kept her eyes on her track shoes. "Which is my room?"

Finding his feet, and his center—the solitary place he always fell back upon—he gestured toward the gold-handled double doors to their right.

"Are my belongings in there?" she asked.

He'd had the bellhop bring her case straight up. He nodded. "Yes."

She hugged herself, a gesture conveying a need for distance. "Then, if you don't mind, it's been a long day. I'd like to take a shower."

He blew out a breath.

Make it a cold one and that's not a bad idea.

Forty minutes later Jenna emerged from her private suite, her hair damp, her creamy skin fresh and radiant. Dressed in a tank top and a pair of faded sweats, the years seemed to melt away. She didn't look a day over twenty.

Decked out in a crisp tuxedo, Gage came in from the balcony and unhooked her surprise, which he'd hung earlier on a curtain rod.

Her expression opened—more disbelief than wonder. She stopped fluffing her hair with the towel. Those pink-polished toes edged another step closer. "What's that?"

"An evening gown."

The dress rustled as he laid it over his arm and moved forward to present it.

"We have seats waiting at an exclusive special event," he told her. "We're going out."

Six

"Mate, why didn't you tell me about her?"

Amidst a room full of tinkling crystal and clinking silverware, Gage slid Nick Farraday a look.

His friend, and second-in-charge in Sydney, pulled in his chin and put up both palms. "I take that back. Your personal life has always been just that—personal. Let me say, though, I feel privileged to be one of the first to meet your bride-to-be." His boyish smile curved upwards. "Jenna and my fiancée seem to have hit it off."

Nick tipped his head toward the ladies who sat, deep in conversation, at the romantically lit table. Tonight's event had been organized to raise funds for cancer research. Seating was intimate. Numbers restricted. Only the wealthiest or most influential in New South Wales had been invited.

The band's swing tune was subdued and pleasant.

On a generous square of timber flooring, set beneath silver moonbeam lights, several couples swayed cheek-to-cheek. Which seemed like a rather good idea.

Earlier Jenna had made herself clear. No sex. No way. However, she hadn't ruled out dancing, which, aside from soothing his wound, would also add another convincing touch to their happy-couple front.

Forcing his gaze away from the delicate curve of Jenna's jaw, Gage focused on the advice he'd given as they'd entered the building's foyer this evening.

If we're to succeed, we must pretend to everyone. No exceptions.

"Jenna and I were meant to be," he told Nick with a sincere smile. "We realized it when we met again after I flew in to pay my respects."

The younger man leant closer and lowered his voice more. "What a tragedy. Her sister, the brother-in-law and her father." Elbow on the chair's arm, he positioned a hand near his mouth and murmured, "Guess there's no need for us to pursue Darley Realty. Your marriage will square that one away. Not that I'm suggesting this engagement has anything to do with that."

About to reply, Gage was interrupted by Nick's fiancée, Summer Reynold. "I'm so excited for you both. Jenna will look like a princess on your wedding day."

She looked like a princess *tonight*.

The woman he'd spoken with earlier today had said the gown was an original from a Brazilian designer's collection. The sleeveless silk bodice was jewel-encrusted, the pleated chiffon skirt falling from high on the waist. In the exclusive boutique's window, the gown appeared to be an ideal fit—long and busty. Guessing

Jenna's shoe size, he'd told the assistant to include matching heels. Both had arrived unexpectedly after Jenna had gone to shower.

The gown hadn't been meant for any specific occasion, however, given this afternoon's awkward interaction, it had seemed wise to avoid confined spaces. Hence the last-minute decision to make use of the tickets he'd arranged for months back and join Nick and Summer this evening.

"I mentioned to Summer that our wedding will be a private ceremony," Jenna explained, her eyes reflecting the lilac folds of the gown. "Not too many guests."

Gage picked up the thread and carried it through. "There'll be just the celebrant, Jenna, myself and two witnesses."

Summer's hand found Nick's on the white tablecloth. "Well, if you're stuck for those two witnesses and we can help..."

Gage smiled. He couldn't be happier for Nick— Summer was a gem. An attractive woman, intelligent and apparently thoughtful. He understood why his friend was so clearly hooked.

He and Nick had met at a convention on the Gold Coast six years ago. Gage had hired him a week later, and Nick had proven many times since then that loyalty was his middle name. On top of that, he and Nick were on the same wavelength, always saw the same picture, big or small, perhaps because they'd both started out with nothing. If Gage had envisaged a brother, Nick would have been him.

Gage poured ice water into Jenna's glass then his own. "As a matter of fact, I would be honored for Nick to be my best man."

Nick's face broke into a wide smile. He stuck out his hand and Gage happily accepted. "With bells on, mate." His grin turned curious. "Want me to arrange for a bachelor's evening?"

"Girls jumping out of cakes and a bawdy night on the town?" Gage grinned back. "You know that's not my style."

Nick raised his glass in salute. "Just checking."

Jenna seemed to freeze for a moment before turning toward Summer. "And I'd love for you to be my maid of honor."

Gage's chest squeezed. Jenna would be thinking of Amy—of how much she'd want her twin by her side on her wedding day, particularly given the reason for this marriage. But who could say that Amy wouldn't be there? Love, and belief, were said to be powerful things.

Summer beamed, took hold of Jenna's hands and drew her up as she pushed to her feet as well. "I'll make sure you look beyond beautiful." They moved off toward the powder room, Summer explaining to Jenna, "I've never been a bridesmaid before. None of my friends are married yet, and I don't have any sisters…"

While Gage kept his eyes glued on Jenna's profile, waiting for her reaction to Summer's last comment, Nick picked up on his train of thought.

"Don't worry, mate. Knowing Summer, she brought up family to give Jenna a chance to mention the accident…or not. She won't push." He exhaled audibly and sat back. "One thing… Jenna's fortunate to have you to look after her father's business now."

Gage sucked air between his teeth. "Jenna wasn't bequeathed Darley Realty."

Nick's forehead creased before a look of compre-hension dawned. "Darley's widow?" Gage nodded and Nick's palm slapped the table. "With mixed families, it can go either way."

Gage flexed his brows. "It went all the way with Leeann Darley."

"Will Jenna contest the will?"

Gage gave a considered reply. "Not that aspect."

"Well, from the way you look at her, I doubt she'll want for a thing, now or any time in the future."

While Nick sipped his wine and focused on the band, tapping his free hand to the tune, Gage wondered. He'd told Jenna the connection they shared was palpable, but did the tug he felt toward Jenna show that much?

He would never enjoy that depth of feeling with anyone else. These past days that enjoyment had grown to such an extent that the sizzle of his early twenties glowed like a kid's birthday candle compared to the twenty-story blaze he'd recently endured.

Of course, now she'd held up the stop sign, and he had to douse the flames. Not easy, but doable.

He downed three parts of his water.

Definitely doable.

Nick turned to him. "Guess I can come clean now, but I never thought I'd see you married. I know you've dated," his eyebrows jumped, "some real beauties, if you don't mind me saying. But you never commented on any of them, and now I know why. Your heart was already taken. Just goes to show. I never pegged you for a romantic."

Gage felt the smile of satisfaction move across his face then shook himself.

Hell, he was believing his own publicity! Yes, Jenna had held a place in his heart no other woman could hope to fill, but that didn't mean he was meant for marriage and a family of his own, not long term, anyway. Whether or not he wished it were different, he was a loner, of necessity living life by his terms and no one else's. When a man married he had to compromise, give up a part of himself. Good luck if he could do that. But Gage knew himself too well. If he tried to pretend to either Jenna or himself that this coming marriage was anything other than pragmatic, someone would get hurt. Again. The whole idea of them being together was to make up for a wrong, not slip up and make matters worse.

Baby Meg could steal anyone's heart. And she deserved someone who could give his heart right back.

Nick swiveled more toward Gage. "I know this probably isn't the time, but did you get in contact with James today? He's been on my case all afternoon."

Gage smothered a twinge of guilt. He'd known James, his right-hand man in Melbourne, had been trying to track him down. He'd turned off his cell phone but there'd been messages left on his hotel extension, on the fax, his email. He hadn't listened to or returned any calls these past days unless they were related to Jenna's situation. Not usual practice. In fact, highly unusual. And unacceptable. He mightn't have had a vacation in too long to remember, but that was no excuse. People relied on him to give 110 percent.

"I'll check in with James tomorrow," he said.

"Just so you know…our Emirates business deal has hit the fan."

Gage's fingers bunched up the tablecloth.

Not possible. "Everything was set."

"Apparently not. I'll let James explain, but he mentioned if you want to keep the deal, you'll need to fly to Dubai ASAP and stay there until the negotiations with the government are settled and stamped."

Gage's mind zeroed in on possible problems and solutions to the billion-dollar hotel contract he'd spent two years putting together. He would jump on his jet first thing tomorrow and—

Laughter caught his ear and jerked that thought clear from his head. The ladies swept back over to the table, chatting like old friends. Gage's fist, and the bunched cloth, relaxed.

Jenna needed friends, people to connect with. And if she and Summer got along, there was every reason to believe they would continue the relationship after…

Well, after he and Jenna had reached their goal and Meg was where, and with whom, she belonged. Where Jenna belonged too. Finally home.

Before Jenna could sit, Gage thought of Dubai, of the limited time they had, and pushed back his chair.

On his feet, he claimed her hand and began to move off. "We should dance."

She pulled back her weight. "Dessert's just arrived." A tilt of her chin indicated the uniformed waiter delivering passion-fruit cheesecake and chocolate torte drizzled with raspberry coulee.

He circled her waist and ushered her away. "Dessert can wait."

Jenna quivered from her head down to her new high heels as Gage took her in his arms and, beneath a shower of smoky light, drew her near.

His left hand rested against the dip in her back. Her mouth went dry when his thumb circled the silky fabric inches above her behind—then stopped. But there was still the smell of him…the raw and tangible heat. The entire package did sinfully sweet things to every dimension of her body. Though he kept his eyes straight ahead, she knew he felt it too.

Question was: after this afternoon's confrontation, could she trust him not to act on it?

His thumb rubbed—stopped again—and Jenna trembled.

Lord, oh, Lord, think of something else.

"Nick's lovely," she blurted out. "I'd imagined a Jerry Maguire type but he's more a Sir Galahad. And Summer's so friendly."

"I'm glad you two get along well."

His chin grazed her temple as he spoke. Clearly he'd used a razor before donning that tux—which happened to fit his body like a Hollywood dream—yet already the shadow and rasp of his beard was evident…and very sexy.

Jenna closed her eyes.

How she yearned for a blank slate to give her peace. Instead pictures of his perfect forearm, from when she'd caught him earlier that day, swam in her mind. Another image followed of the coarse hair below the hollow of his throat. Today, directly after Gage's admission, how dearly she'd wanted to reach out and rub those crisp strands against his hot, tanned skin. She almost had.

Above the music, his deep voice infiltrated her daydream. "That was nice."

She heard the smile in his voice. Then guilt convulsed in her throat and her eyes flew open. She inched away from the hard plateau under his dress shirt, the masculine lure of his hips.

"Sorry, what did you say?"

His brow buckled before amusement hooked up one side of his mouth. "Asking Summer to be your maid of honor," he explained. "That was nice."

She sighed and smiled. "Oh. That."

His brow wrinkled again while his own smile widened. "What did you think I meant?"

The press of his hand on her back increased so subtly, she might have imagined it. Of course, she might not have imagined it either.

Her gaze skated over to the band.

Subject change—*quick.*

"I love this song."

She felt the heat of his eyes on her, trying to penetrate her veneer. "So I was right in asking you to dance."

She inwardly groaned. The simmering effects of slow dancing did little to strengthen the answer she'd given to his tempting but unacceptable suggestion this afternoon.

She cocked her head and thought more deeply.

But he wasn't acting improperly now. Merely adding to the picture they were building on. Reunited lovers. The we-simply-couldn't-deny-our-feelings-any-longer façade.

At least it was supposed to be a façade.

He rocked her around in a tight circle. When they returned to more regular steps, she was closer, the bodice of her gown touching his shirt. Through the sheer fabric, the tips of her breasts rubbed rhythmically back and forth, and when he threw in a fancy one-two-three, they rubbed a little harder.

The points of contact began to burn. The burn became an ache.

She broke from his hold.

Enough!

"I think we should eat dessert," she told him firmly.

He cut such an impressive picture, silver beams of light casting shadows over the chiseled planes of his face and dynamite cut of his tux. Without a scrap of effort, his presence dominated the massive room. The energy of his masculinity was lawless.

And dangerously close to irresistible.

He smiled as his hand reached for hers. "Our dance isn't over."

She gave him a wide berth.

Oh, yes it is.

Heartbeat clamoring, she wove through a field of besotted couples to find their table.

This was much worse than she first thought. Now that she knew his mind—that he wanted her in his bed—it wasn't enough that she'd made a choice. No matter how he tempted her, she couldn't jeopardize her chance with Meg by getting mixed up with Gage on a sexual level. She needed to be sharp, not lovelorn. And yet…

After just one dance, her breasts were on fire and her mind was spinning like a top. All her poor brain could register was the agony-ecstasy of being embraced by the only man who could make her feel like a woman should feel. Desirable, unique. Wanted…cherished… every inch…every minute.

The waves of arousal that had swamped her in her teens were back with a devastating vengeance. Yet, if she gave in to the pleasure and allowed herself to be carried away, no doubt about it—she would drown. Twelve years ago she'd come close to sinking, and the stakes were far higher this time.

She smiled as warmly as she could at Summer and Nick and folded back into her seat.

Summer's spoon fell against her dish with a *click*. "Well, that was the world's quickest dance."

Gage appeared and pulled his chair in, too. "Seems my skills on the dance floor can't compete with my fiancée's sweet tooth." He gave his napkin a sharp flick and set it on his lap.

Nick slid Summer a questioning look. Summer conveyed a secret shrug. Gage downed the rest of his water and Jenna shifted in her seat.

Awkward moment.

"If I recall correctly, you have a sweet tooth, too, Gage," Jenna injected brightly to cover everyone's discomfort. He opened his mouth to speak but Jenna talked over him. "Now, don't deny it."

A muscle in his jaw clenched as Gage slid his plate closer. "I was about to say you were the one who changed my mind. I didn't think I liked dessert until I met you."

Jenna went limp.

She watched him sample the torte, suck some cream off his thumb, and got the strongest feeling his line wasn't the least manufactured. One week after they'd first kissed all those years ago, she'd bought a tub of ice cream to share while they watched TV in the pool house—their after-hours hideaway. He'd told her he didn't like sweet food, only savory—steak, potatoes, thick crusty bread. He simply was not interested in toffee brittle or cupcakes.

But she'd pounced and force-fed him a mouthful of premium French vanilla. Laughing, he'd rolled her off his chest, then swallowed and finally hummed out a big smile.

He'd been so sure about not liking sweets…but a week together and she'd changed his mind.

"Something wrong with your cheesecake?"

At Summer's murmured question, Jenna brought herself back. She focused on her plate and inhaled the tangy scent of passion-fruit pulp. "I'm sure it's delicious."

Gage dabbed his mouth and kicked off a conversation with Nick regarding the strength of the Australian dollar against the greenback. He drew Summer, a leading chartered accountant, into the conversation, too.

A chill crept up Jenna's spine.

Was he giving her the cold shoulder, annoyed that she'd left him on the dance floor? Or was he frustrated over her unwillingness this afternoon to let him clarify his feelings more fully? Had he changed his mind? Not about ice cream this time, but about spending the rest of his life alone?

Nick's voice came from far away. "Mate, she doesn't look too well."

"Perhaps we should call it a night," Summer suggested.

Jenna touched her forehead and found it damp. Her smile quivered. "Maybe I shouldn't have had that second glass of champagne with dinner."

But champagne bubbles hadn't lit the fires sparking through her system. A different, unanticipated new spin on things had.

Gage tipped close. "Would you like to leave?"

She nodded then spoke to Nick and Summer. "Sorry to be a bore."

Nick got to his feet. "Not at all. We can do this again soon."

Summer stood too and kissed Jenna's cheek as she rose. "In just under three weeks, in fact. But we won't be eating torte that day. It'll be a scrumptious wedding cake."

They all left the building together. Nick and Summer slipped into a cab while Gage turned in the direction of his penthouse.

But Jenna held back. "Do you mind if we go for a walk?" A blush singed her cheeks as he studied her, and she added, "I could do with the fresh air."

"You won't be cold?"

Little chance of that with her internal furnace working at maximum capacity whenever he was near.

She smiled. "I'll be fine."

They strolled in silence down a busy city street, headlights flashing in their faces and the Harbour Bridge twinkling like an arc of supernova stars in the distance. Within minutes, they reached Darling Harbour. Al fresco restaurants hummed with life while, farther down, the replica of Captain Cook's *Endeavour* sat quietly moored outside the Maritime Museum.

The wind picked up, flapping the massive sails and swirling around Jenna's hem.

Gage shrugged out of his jacket and draped it over her bare shoulders. "Don't argue," he chided when she went to object. "The breeze is chilly coming off the water."

Standing behind her, he positioned the jacket's big shoulders to fit her far smaller ones.

"Thank you." She hugged the jacket close, taking secret pleasure in the male scented warmth enveloping her. "And thanks for the lovely evening. I had a nice time."

"I'm glad you enjoyed Nick and Summer's company."

"I enjoyed your company, too."

A dark eyebrow lifted. "As long as I don't get too close," he observed as they resumed walking.

She tingled, remembering his arms around her, his granite chest and sizzling body heat so agonizingly tempting. What was the safe answer?

She decided there wasn't one.

The diamond on her finger flashed beneath the city lights and she found herself smiling.

"Jenna Cameron… It has a nice ring to it." She'd always thought so.

"Cameron was my mother's maiden name."

Jenna felt a stab of pain for him—over the loss of his mother, growing up without a father, of being unable to share a father's name.

"I didn't know that," she murmured.

He nodded. "Whenever my mother had one too many and got out the old snaps, she'd insist that our line of Camerons had descended from kings." He chuckled and kicked a pebble with the toe of his polished lace-up shoe.

"Perhaps it's true," she said, but his wry smile said he doubted it. "Have you ever tried to look up your family tree?"

His smile changed. "You're kidding, right?"

She took him in, the uncompromising jut of his jaw, the lock of inky hair lifting in the salty breeze. "You might discover she's right and you do have royal blood in your veins."

That might help explain his exceptional abilities as a leader.

"More likely I'm descended from convicts. Only took a dozen generations to crawl our way out of the squalor."

He grinned but she didn't see humor in the single line bracketing his mouth.

"Guess it doesn't matter where we came from. Just who we turn out to be."

He stopped just as a cloud swallowed up the moonlight. "Jenna, where we come from *is* who we are."

"If that were true, you'd be wearing some type of crown or dragging chains."

"Yes," he said, "I would."

Dropping his gaze, he kicked another pebble. It skipped clear across the ground and plopped in the water. Needing a little time to think over his last remark, she followed it toward the water's edge, but he called her back.

"Hey, I thought we were walking."

She shrugged. "I walked over here."

"I prefer dry land. Blame the psychogenetic memory of great, great granddaddy locked in the hull of that convict ship. I don't think he could swim, either."

She laughed. "I promise not to push you in."

His arms raveled over his chest.

Jenna grinned.

Stubborn man.

She moved back and, equally determined, set her hands on her hips. When her elbows jutted, the jacket dislodged. Jenna grabbed to save it, but Gage moved first. He caught the sleeves, pinning them against her upper arms. The action also drew her in and toward him—wonderfully, dangerously close.

With his chest inches from hers, he searched her eyes. Her toes curled as sensual longing ignited a sizzling trail through her body. It was all she could do not to press a little closer, a little harder.

"Let's keep walking," she murmured, and then to ease the tension, "You can impress me with your knowledge of yachts."

"I know nothing about yachts." But he loosened his hold, rounded the jacket up over her shoulders, and they began to walk down the pier.

"You don't have a hundred-foot cruiser?" She'd seen pictures of the excessive luxury available on such vessels. Surely Gage would have one or two documented on his assets list.

"I don't like water, remember? Italian sports cars, corporate jets, no problem. Boats? Not even a little bit."

She hadn't given it much thought at the time, but whenever he'd visited her at the pool house years ago, he had always stayed well clear of the pool itself. He really didn't like water? But why? There must be some good reason.

The pocket of his jacket buzzed—his cell phone. Jenna grinned. As if he would ever leave that behind.

After asking permission, he dug into a pocket and checked the cell's screen. "Excuse me." He thumbed a button. "This is important."

As he spoke—something about Dubai—she breathed in the briny air, examined the rows of vessels and stole sidelong glances at his profile, wondering. Maybe even hoping.

Phone pressed between his shoulder and ear, Gage asked permission again to rummage through his jacket. This time he retrieved a pen and scribbled a few words on his hand. Another few seconds and he disconnected.

"Guess the Cameron shop never shuts down," she said.

He reread the message on his hand. "I've neglected a few matters."

He was about to slot the pen away, but it flashed in a pier light and, on impulse, Jenna reached for it. He seemed reluctant to give it up.

She weighed the pen in her palm. "Hmm, heavy. It's not pure gold, is it?" His expression was noncommittal and she looked closer. "It *is* pure gold."

"That's not so unusual."

"Maybe not for you. What's this?" She rotated the pen and squinted in the hazy light. "An inscription? No. A symbol of some kind." She passed over it with her fingertip. "A vertical line with an arc at one end. It's a tree. Or an anchor."

"It's a plane. Why would I buy a pen with an anchor etched on it?"

She rolled her eyes theatrically. "Oh, that's right. You don't like water. But you do like jets." And your Maserati. Leading examples of speed and power.

He reached for the pen. Unprepared, she fumbled and it fell then bounced on the rough decking. Gage swooped and caught it a second before it might have rolled off into the harbour, lost forever.

Horrified, Jenna's hands flew to her mouth. "Gage, I'm so sorry."

He rose from his haunches. "No harm done. I would've hated to see you jump in there to get it though."

When he grinned, so did she.

But her smile faded. "It means a lot to you, doesn't it?"

He slipped the pen into his trouser pocket. "I bought it on a whim after a stock market gain, and signed my first big contract with it. I used it constantly until it started to wear. Now I generally keep it for important documents."

Yet he carried it around with him even when there were no contracts in sight? "Sounds like that pen is your good luck charm." And quite possibly more than that…a connection.

He shrugged. "Either way, I don't want to lose it."

"The pen with the plane, not the anchor or tree."

He winked. "Now you're catching on."

"Am I?"

As their gazes held, the atmosphere changed from relaxed to suddenly steamy. The heavy weight of lost years shrank and crystallized into a single, bright, hypercharged moment.

Was she reading too much into how adamantly he defended what that pen represented? Wealth, travel, independence, freedom. All the things he'd let her know were important to him a week ago.

Ice cream was one thing, life choices another. And, no matter how much she secretly wished it were otherwise, Gage seemed set on his choices. Beyond that? He was quite simply a magnificent enigma. No matter how many times she second-guessed herself, she would never know Gage Cameron. The reality was—to try might mean her downfall.

A cold, wet drop fell on Jenna's nose. At the same moment lightning flashed and a roll of distant thunder rumbled. Distracted, she looked up, and as if on cue, the rain came down.

When she shrieked, Gage swept the jacket over her head. A second later, he cursed and also ducked under cover.

While his arms made an awkward umbrella of the jacket, her palm landed against the hard wall of his chest. His heartbeat resonated through her fingers then spread like an electric current through her body. Crazy, and yet, for the first time in too long, she felt…safe.

His big shoulders were hunched. "We're soaked through."

She grinned. "I noticed."

"You said you wouldn't make me swim."

She grinned more, then couldn't help but think, *Would it really be so scary to swim, Gage? Couldn't you get used to it?*

This seemed the ideal as well as the most inappropriate moment to ask. "Why do you have such an aversion to water?"

"Ever wonder about the scar on my lip? I knocked three of my baby teeth out when I was washed down a storm pipe at age five. On top of swallowing a whole lot of mud, I almost drowned."

Jenna gasped. She couldn't imagine how terrified he must have been. "Did you ever think of seeing a professional to help you get over your fear?"

He smiled in grim amusement. "Avoidance has worked very well up till now."

Yet they continued to stand in the downpour, beneath the jacket. They should have run for shelter, but neither one moved while the rain pounded at their feet and his heart thudded near her palm.

"Jenna?"

In the dark, she imagined his mouth was incredibly close. "Yes, Gage?"

He seemed to move nearer.

She did the same....

Seven

Standing in the pouring rain, both huddled beneath his tuxedo jacket, the reality was unavoidable. Gage was going to kiss her.

How would she react? Jenna couldn't think past the frantic beating of her heart, or the way her every fiber cried out for him to do it *now*.

She held her breath, waiting…

Then Gage groaned deeply and took her hand. "We've had enough fresh air."

The jacket came down and they ran off together, splashing through the puddles.

Ten minutes later, they entered the penthouse, shaking their wet hands and slipping off sodden shoes.

"Can I get you a towel? Something warm to drink?" Gage crossed to the bar, threw the drenched jacket over the back of a stool and reached for a crystal decanter. He poured himself two fingers in a heavy glass. No ice.

A convulsive shudder rippled up Jenna's spine. She was freezing, but a hot chocolate would suit her far better than scotch.

She inspected the puddle forming around her feet. "I think I'll change before anything else."

He thumbed a switch on a wall panel—the internal heating, she suspected—and downed half his single malt.

His shirt was plastered against the musculature of his deeply tanned chest and arms. Every knockout ridge and bulge was on display, presented in glorious prime-time relief. As he moved forward, more than the line between his brows told her he was uncomfortable. At being caught in the rain, ending up sopping wet? Or something, perhaps, not quite as obvious.

When they'd taken shelter beneath his jacket, he'd almost kissed her. Worse, she'd almost let him.

And he knew it.

Closer now, he lifted his chin to unravel his bow tie and flick open a button.

"It's getting late." He stopped before her. "Guess you're tired."

He took another quick sip and swallowed, waiting for her reply. Waiting for a sign. A look.

A touch.

She should go and change, yet she stood immobile, thinking of the heartache she'd lived through when she'd known Gage Cameron last. His life wasn't one she could ever share. And yet…had she changed her mind about becoming intimately involved? Down by the pier, she'd been tempted. Heck, she was tempted now.

Guess you're tired.

She gave a cryptic reply. "That sprint seems to have woken me up."

His eyes searched hers. "Me, too."

Behind him, the facsimile machine beeped. His gaze flicked over her face before he moved to retrieve a sheet from the tray. After scanning the message, he set down his drink and ran a hand through his glossy wet hair.

She inched closer. "Is it the Dubai problem again?"

Jaw clenched, he nodded at the page. "Sorry. You get changed. I need a moment here." He sank into a chair, found a pen on the desk and started making notes.

Jenna let out a sigh.

Perhaps she should take his reaction to this fax as a sign. He gave a good impression of a dedicated fiancé, but Gage would always be devoted to business.

He'd go for the plane, not the anchor, every time.

It should be enough that he'd offered to help her with Meg, and that he still found her desirable, although not at the moment. Head down, concentrating on the fax, he looked set for the duration.

Raising her dripping hem, Jenna padded a barefoot trail over the cold tiles into her carpeted room. She stripped off the dress and inspected it for damage; into the dry cleaners tomorrow, first thing.

After changing into the men's shirt she preferred to a negligee, the laptop caught her eye. She sat down and found her email inbox full. Proposals for overseas work, a free offer from a shoe store, a message from Leeann…

Her heart jackknifed into her throat and her shaky finger slipped over the mouse to click the message open straight away.

Letting you know, I've had to step up my plans to visit San Fran. My poor mother is ailing and begging to see our Meg. Back after Christmas—all going well.

That crippling, hopeless feeling gripped as if it had never been away.

All going well, be damned! Leeann had no intention of returning after Christmas.

It was happening, just as she'd feared. Leeann was leaving the country with Meg, for how long, she couldn't hope to guess. And what the hell could she do about it? Nothing. A big fat zero. As far as the law was concerned, Leeann was Meg's rightful guardian.

A light appeared in the darkness and she pushed to her feet.

Gage would know what to do.

She flew out the door. He hadn't moved.

"She's taking Meg away," she shot out. "I don't know when exactly, but she won't be in a hurry to bring her back. Maybe we should go see her. Petition for a special hearing or something."

Anything. Just as long as it was soon.

Gage pushed to his feet and braced her shoulders. "Slow down. What do you mean, taking Meg?"

Unshed tears stung her nose. Yes, she should stay calm—not exactly easy given the bloody great pit gaping before her.

Grabbing his hand, Jenna headed for her room. "Read for yourself."

In her room, Gage concentrated on the screen while Jenna paced back and forth.

"She has no intention of coming back," she said, pressing her throbbing temple. "Not until she's good and ready anyway. It's no use me flying over there to see Meg. Why would she let me through the door? I doubt the American police would be too eager to get involved in this kind of custody issue. She'd be in total control."

The way Leeann always liked it.

Jenna thought of Amy's gift to her on their fifteenth birthday. Leeann had fallen in love with the beautiful lovebird too—everyone had. One day Jenna returned home from school to find Tulip's birdcage not in her bedroom but the family room. A week later, the cage had migrated to Leeann's sitting room. Their father had intervened—the first of only two occasions. The following month, Leeann had taken it upon herself to clean the cage and Tulip had "accidentally" escaped. Over time, Jenna had replaced her hurt with a vengeful wish: soon she would fly away too. And never ever come back.

Gage straightened from where he leant on the back of her chair and rapped his knuckles several times against his outer thigh. Jenna's gaze scanned up from the movement. Her pulse rate tripled and mouth went dry. Some segment of her consciousness must have noticed, yet it hadn't registered until now. He'd discarded his wet dress shirt. From the hips up, he was naked—bronzed. Unbelievably built.

"Don't panic," he said. "It's more likely she's being manipulative and trying to call our bluff. *Give me what I want or you might not see your niece again.*"

Jenna wet her lips. "You mean she's threatening us?" Well, that made sense.

In the muted lamplight, she watched him grin. "But her threat carries no weight. She won't find another buyer for Darley Realty in the state it's in. She'd have more than enough to get her to the States, but if she wants real money, she needs to listen, not talk."

His drying hair was disheveled as if, while they'd been in separate rooms, his fingers had thrust through its thick crop several times. The unruly look suited him as much as it had in his youth, if not more.

Jenna shook herself and connected her runaway thoughts to Meg's situation.

"So, if Leeann takes the deal—Meg in exchange for an easy, generous sale—we don't need to get married."

Despite the silly pang of disappointment, that had to be a good thing.

Right?

Expression earnest, he took her hands and squeezed. "Jenna, we not only need to get married, we need to do it quickly and get that petition in and fast-tracked for the earliest possible hearing. If there's one thing I've learned it's wherever possible, don't put all your eggs in one basket."

In other words, despite his assurances, he wasn't certain what Leeann would do.

"So if she decides having Meg means more to her than the money…then if a judge decides to abide by the will's directives…"

She thought of Meg…of her little bird…

He brought her hands to his chest and pressed them close. "That won't happen."

His words, and steady strumming of his heart, brooked no argument.

But she couldn't be a Pollyanna now. If she kept thinking about it, rehashing all the options, making alternate plans…maybe if she prayed hard enough, long enough, God wouldn't let this happen.

Hot tears welled in her eyes. "But what if it *does* happen?"

What if this were punishment for her willfulness? If she'd put her family first and pride last, she would have stayed in Australia. She would be settled, Amy and Brad would've put her name in their wills and Meg wouldn't be stuck with a guardian who'd turned into the worst kind of witch.

Gage thumbed aside her tear as it trickled down her cheek. "It won't happen. We'll find a way."

Her mind jumped again.

"And how long do we try? A month, a year, two, ten?" How long before Meg began to see Leeann as her parent? At some point it would be unfair to take her from the person she'd come to see as her mother, no matter how unworthy.

When a small sob escaped, Gage wrapped his arms around her, and Jenna remembered a time when he had been all that she'd needed. She inhaled his clean musky scent, and her hands slid up to the broad flat rocks that defined his chest.

He felt so good. Made her feel so safe.

His hand smoothed over her hair then he murmured against her head. "One day at a time. I'll fix it. Trust me."

She scrunched her burning eyes shut.

Can I trust you, Gage? Can I trust myself?

His mouth grazed her temple, then again and again.

After a long moment, he held her even tighter and said, "I'm here. We'll sort this out tomorrow."

She lifted her face and, yes, his supportive smile *was* there. But along with that look came awareness—the same intense knowledge that had always pulsed and steamed between them. His expression changed and the heat of his body, pressed against hers, built until she could barely breathe.

His head lowered slightly, hers tipped up, then his mouth was closing over hers...taking her...kissing her...*thank God,* finally.

She was already melting when he broke from their embrace.

He stepped back, the cords in his neck strained. "You're upset. You need to rest."

She shook her head. "Right now what I need is you."

Ready to be kissed again and forget her problems, if only for a moment, she offered up her lips.

He held her back and groaned as he'd done beneath the jacket in the rain. "Damn it, Jenna, right now what you want is a friend, not a lover."

It was easy to read between the lines: He was telling her he wouldn't take advantage of her when she was emotionally vulnerable. Just as he wouldn't think of taking advantage of a woman who'd had too much to drink.

Or was under age, as she'd once been.

In the pool house that night, she'd begged him to go all the way. She'd felt his body lock and tremble above her, his physical need doing hellish battle with his scruples. She'd cursed him when he'd left Sydney without a word, and yet there was a noble deed to acknowledge too: Now she could admit that he'd respected her enough not to take what he wanted and screw the consequences.

But she was no longer a teen. She was an adult facing the biggest challenge of her life. She knew what she was doing here, tonight, and now nothing stopped them from finally enjoying it.

If she did lose Meg…

No! She couldn't bear to even *think* it, and she had the perfect diversion—making love to the only man she'd ever wanted…would ever want. Arms looping around his neck, she pulled herself up and set the tip of her nose to his.

"Forget what I said this afternoon. I want this. And I get it, Gage. I get *you*. You don't want to grow roots, and you don't want to take advantage of me. Thank you, but believe me when I say, no regrets, I promise. Like you said, let's finally just find out."

She angled her head and this time *she* kissed *him*.

The tension left his jaw. With a soft inner smile, she shimmied nearer and welcomed his full surrender. But he'd already taken the lead, deepening the kiss as his hands slid a sensuous path from where he cupped her face to the curve of her neck, then lower, sculpting the tingling slope of her shoulders.

When his hot palms skimmed down the full length of her arms, her shirt—and total submission—came, too.

Eight

Any reservations Gage had evaporated like a blast of high-powered steam.

Jenna had a change of heart and now everything seemed perfectly clear…the wonderful way she felt in his arms, the wild berry scent of her filling his lungs, filling him with life. He could go on kissing her till doomsday, but for one tiny problem.

Other delights should be shared aside from kissing, and tonight he intended for them to enjoy every one.

As he carefully turned her to face away from him, the oversized shirt, which he'd already slipped from her shoulders, fell completely from her body. He scooped his arms up under hers and crossed them over her ribs. Then he closed his eyes, created an image in his mind, and lovingly molded his palms over her breasts as a dedicated artist might test and shape his work. They were fuller than he remembered—heavier, but just as beautiful…and even more arousing.

With a sigh—a sound of pure pleasure—she reached up and back to coax his head down. As he kissed her neck, her fingers wound through his hair. "I've dreamt about you so often, but this is a hundred times better."

He smiled at her admission. "Only a hundred times?" He rolled her nipples.

She quivered and sighed again. "Make that a thousand. A *million*."

"Now we're getting close."

His palms grazed a wide circle across each peak before slowly riding down over her ribs, his fingers forming arrows tracking toward the juncture of her thighs. As his chest grazed down her back, his lips trailed the scented curve between ear and shoulder, and his hands discovered her inner thighs; his pulse rate spiraled as his thumbs delved between to gently edge them apart. He pressed her firmly against his pelvis then rode his touch higher, between her slick soft folds.

She was so ready. And he was way beyond ready for her.

Finding that hypersensitive spot, he began to work some heartfelt magic and her lower half tipped forward. When he increased the pressure, varied the motion, she started to move, a sensual, barely perceptible roll of her hips.

The heat between them rose and her movements grew bolder until she stilled then trembled, her energy and concentration obviously strung piano-wire tight. Time to pull back. He wanted this to last. Although she was close, ultimately she would appreciate that kind of delay, too.

They had all night.

As he eased her back around to face him, an appetizing thought struck. He cupped her bottom and nipped her lower lip. "So, you don't wear panties to bed."

Her eyes were dark and drowsy with desire. "I didn't know that was a crime."

"Not if I'd been around to enjoy the benefits."

Her grin was mischievous. "That sentiment works both ways."

He felt a tug and looked down.

She'd helped herself to his zipper.

The fly came down, her hand went in and the testosterone explosion almost took off his head.

This woman was bold, as she'd been all those years ago, but now there was no hint of fumbling or blushing. Jenna seemed to know precisely what she was doing and how she would do it.

A vision came to mind but he stomped on it quickly. He couldn't think of her with anyone else. He would only think of now—not the past, or the future—because this very minute that big empty space was finally filling with light.

Tonight he felt reborn.

He swept her off her feet at the same moment his unzipped trousers fell. He stepped from the pooled legs and carried his fiancée to bed.

As he walked, he kissed her, long and slow and deep, with every ounce of feeling he'd ever boxed in. Then he laid her on the sheets and watched her glow in the lamplight, dark-blond hair arced over white satin pillows, her lips slightly parted, wet and inviting.

When he was completely naked, he lay beside her and finally pulled her close. As one long shapely leg eased up to hook over his hip, he took her mouth again and her arched foot on his behind urged him on. Not that he needed persuading. His blood was on fire, every cell in his body ablaze with a desire that would devour every inch of her before coming even halfway close to containment.

Their kiss broke down into desperate snatches, his mouth tracking over her jaw, down her rain-scented neck and lower, until he dotted airy kisses over one perfect breast then the other.

She fisted her fingers in his hair as she writhed beneath him. "You need to know…you're driving me insane."

He didn't stop, or slow, or even think. He merely smiled as the tip of his tongue tickled her nipple. When the peak was hard and distended, his teeth grazed and gently tugged. Then, at long last, he drew the cherry into his mouth, burning the memory of sublime pleasure into his heart and mind forever.

Arching toward him, she whispered something half decipherable and incredibly sexy. His pounding erection hardened to stone. When her knee edged higher on his hip, he clutched her leg and ran his tongue all the way down her middle, lowering himself over her body and the bed until he landed smack-dab in heaven.

She tasted exactly as he'd imagined…fresh and provocatively feminine. He fanned her thighs wider, settled in and focused on making her happy.

He smiled at her reaction.

Yes, he was definitely making her happy.

All too soon, the pressure in his groin pulled mercilessly tight. Given the way her fingers dug into his shoulders, Jenna was teetering on a crumpling edge, too.

Summoning control, he pushed up and leaned over to rummage in the bedside drawer. She moved beneath him, her body inching lower as she trailed moist lips across his ribs, down around his navel, lower still until she hit solid rock.

Sweat broke out beneath his shoulder blades and at the backs of his knees. Swallowing a curse, he bit his lip and with a single arm dragged her all the way back up. The tit-for-tat she had in mind would be a wonderful encore, but right now he was too close to the finale.

In the drawer, he found a small square wrapper. Hovering on top, an elbow either side of her head, he captured her mouth again and blindly tore the foil. Her arms wound up, she took the condom, rolled him over and proceeded to fit it while he could only stare.

"You need a hand with anything?"

All done, she slid a python grip down his shaft. "Isn't instinct a marvelous thing?"

Instinct? Did she mean practice?

He wished he'd been the first. But he'd given up the chance, and the better part of him didn't regret it. Once she'd been forbidden fruit. Not now. Now nothing was out of bounds.

He flipped her onto her back and growled, "My turn to take charge."

Blood on fire, he eased inside, but only the barest amount. Nibbling her earlobe, he moved, repositioned and tried again.

His curious smile nuzzled into her neck. "Relax. This is fun, remember?"

Her thighs loosened their clamp outside of his.

"I'm relaxed."

Her answer sounded sincere enough. To be fair, she

was narrow through the hips, a very slender build. Rubbers were sometimes restrictive. Hell, perhaps unconsciously she was still a little nervous.

It wasn't possible that…hell, she couldn't be…

He drew back slightly and smiled into her eyes. "This is going to sound completely crazy, but please tell me this isn't your first time."

"I've been with men before." She pressed her lips together. "Just not this far."

A *virgin?*

After the initial shock, he gathered himself. In this day and age, with her looks and worldly experience—not to mention the way she'd rolled on that condom—not likely.

He chuckled. "You're pulling my leg." His smile wavered. "Aren't you?"

"I've had relationships. A few times I came close to going all the way, but I always pulled back. It never felt right. But this feels right." She slid a fingertip over his bottom lip. "*Very* right."

He looked at her for a long, disbelieving moment then exhaled hard. "Well, this is an unexpected turn of events."

"Does it make a difference?"

He lifted his brows. "Not in a bad way, believe me."

Her fingertip trailed around his jaw, down his neck. "Then what are we waiting for?"

He smiled. *What, indeed?*

Running a hand down her side, he offered up his thoughts to a higher plane and maneuvered again. In time, the rhythm increased, the way became smoother and the friction built from shooting sparks to leaping white-blue flames. When she pulled down on his ears to kiss him again, a bone-melting inferno rushed through his body and the pent-up passion of twelve years exploded and broke free.

She cried out when he drove in to the hilt. Then every muscle in her body seemed to clench and she cried out in a different way. Through a haze of physical intensity and a shuddering soul-lifting release, he felt her spasm around him and knew she'd climaxed, too.

Heartbeat booming, Gage dropped his head near her ear and almost uttered the words—the ones he never said. But in time, he swallowed them back down. He'd finally made love to the only woman who'd ever mattered to him. He'd be content with that.

Afterward he held her nestled in one arm, her head resting against his chest, her hand curled beneath her chin.

She looked up at him, her eyelids heavy, her expression dreamy and satisfied. "Will you be here in the morning when I wake up?"

He thought of the fax and the pieces of the Dubai deal that had already hit ground zero. So much money on the line. Years of work at stake. He needed to fly over there. He was a complete fool if he didn't. And yet...

Hell's fire, he couldn't leave her. Not now, after that manipulative message from Leeann. He'd given his word. This time he would stay.

He bundled her closer and dropped a kiss on her brow. "I'll be here."

But thirty minutes later, when she'd fallen asleep, he eased away and quietly moved into the main living room. If he wasn't going to Dubai, Nick sure as hell had to.

After ripping out a fax sheet, he grabbed a pen.

About to write, he frowned, tossed the Bic and moved back into the bedroom to dig around in his trouser pocket. When he stood over his desk again, the gold pen in his hand, part of the tension and uncertainty eased from his body.

The fax was almost through when a movement caught his eye. Jenna stood in the bedroom doorway, dressed again in that shirt, one arm stretched lazily above her as she yawned.

Her voice was a sleepy sexy drawl. "Are you coming back to bed?"

The fax beeped. Finished.

Exhaling, he set down his pen and joined her. He gathered the hem of that shirt and dragged it over her head in one fluid motion. "There's a rule I insist you abide by while you're living in my home. No men's shirts."

She half frowned, half smiled. "But I don't wear negligees to bed."

Or panties.

He shut the door. "Perfect."

Nine

A week later, Jenna gazed unseeing—barely feeling—past the passenger window of Gage's black Maserati.

The powerful V8 engine hummed around her as, concentrating, Gage navigated the curves and dips of the northbound road. After a recent spring shower, the rural scenery looked lush and fresh. The midmorning sun scattered tiny diamonds across the trees and threw a pail of iridescent green over the gently rolling hills.

Under different circumstances she'd have enjoyed the experience—a leisurely drive with a handsome billionaire, who also happened to be an incredible lover and her husband of three days, no less.

Her engagement ring and matching diamond wedding band shone up from her clasped hands, their brilliance smudged through a blur of tears.

Was she kidding herself? Had marrying Gage really helped her chances of claiming Meg?

Gage reached to squeeze her hand. "Tired? It's been a busy few days. Hours of travel," he flicked over a warm smile, "with a wedding thrown in."

Despite her request that they marry in Australia, as a safeguard Gage had also lodged the necessary paperwork in New Zealand. With documents in order, they'd flown into Wellington, then on to Mt. Ruapehu. The chateau was a combination of early twentieth century elegance and secluded romantic retreat. In a grand room, decorated with fountains of fragrant lilies and pink satin bows, they'd said their vows, Summer and Nick smiling on.

No one would have guessed they weren't in love. When he'd said I do, even she had believed it—a bittersweet sensation that Jenna tried not to dwell upon. Just as she'd tried not to think about Meg every minute of every day.

Not happening. Even now that heavy, helpless feeling pressed down, crushing her, squeezing the air from her lungs. If only she knew when and how this would end. If only she knew when she would hold her Meg—Amy's baby—again.

Gage seemed to read her mind. "Lance hopes to hear back next week about the petition he lodged for us yesterday with the Family Court."

He'd reassured her of this six times already. Gage's lawyer had filed their petition as a married couple, stating that—given Leeann's intention to leave the country and the age of the child—their case was urgent. Plans were advancing as quickly as possible. Leeann was now fully aware of their objectives. But...

Jenna gazed out the window again. "I just wish Leeann would stop playing her games and let me see her."

An image of Meg's rosebud mouth and big blue eyes was a constant in her mind. She'd heard enough excuses. She was at a point where she wanted to knock down Leeann's door and demand to see her niece. Not wise, but oh-so-tempting.

A few minutes later, Gage turned onto a narrower road. But hadn't she seen a letterbox at the corner? Jenna glanced back over her shoulder. And what was the story with that mile-long brick and iron fence?

She frowned. "This is someone's driveway." A very long driveway at that.

Listening to a blues CD, he tapped a thumb on the steering wheel. "Actually, it's our driveway."

Jenna blinked several times. "Ours?"

"This property is our country retreat," he explained. "Yours, mine and Meg's."

Jenna's jaw unhinged as his words sank in and a sprawling ranch-style home came into view. Timber and dark brick, a triple garage, colorful casual gardens and—

Her breath caught then she closed her eyes tight and dropped her head.

He was trying to keep her hopes up, and have an appropriate address for the judge—acreage where a child could run free and play, rather than a multistory penthouse in the central business district. But seeing an extravagant swing set was too much to bear. Would Meg ever use that bright blue slide, or climb through that candy-red cubby house?

Would Jenna ever become her mother?

The car pulled up on the circular drive directly outside the front door.

She let out a long breath. "I know you're trying to be kind…"

"I'm merely being prepared," he replied, easing out of the car.

Preparing for a dream to come true. Well, the biggest part of her dream anyway—gaining guardianship of Meg. She'd always known Gage wasn't a permanent part of the equation. And she could accept that—even after sharing his bed.

Really, she could.

He helped her out and onto the crushed pebble drive. His mouth hooked up at one side. "Want to have a look around?"

He looked better than incredible in that chambray shirt and pair of deep blue jeans. Although his chest was broader and the fine lines branching from his eyes confirmed he was older, the memories flooded back. Once, when he'd worn jeans every day, she'd fantasized about them owning a home together. She'd envisaged a child as well…maybe two. She'd been so in love with him then.

Her chest lurched.

Don't think about that.

As they walked off, Gage wrapped his arm around her waist. "Looks like we have visitors."

Jenna caught sight of another vehicle, parked on the other side of the garages.

Gage was a mystery in many ways, but he could also be thoughtful. He must have asked Nick and Summer out for the day. Summer had been so supportive in New Zealand and had phoned nearly every day since. The company of that lovely couple could be just what the doctor ordered.

But when two people appeared from around the corner, Jenna's smile slipped and the blood from her head funneled straight down to her toes.

Their visitors weren't Summer and Nick.

Gage's question came in a husky murmur at her ear. "Aren't you going to say hello?"

Dazed, she gaped at him. His expression was warmer than she'd ever seen it and his gray eyes…they were dancing!

Tina—Meg's nanny—stopped before them, the baby, in a soft pink and white dress and booties, asleep in her arms. The tiny matching bonnet had slipped and sat slightly crooked on her crown.

"She should be waking soon." Tina smiled down at Meg, who seemed so much bigger since the last time Jenna had seen her. "Maybe we could go inside. It's starting to get hot out here."

While Jenna struggled with rising tears of joy, and a clashing jumble of emotions—*How long do I have her? How hard will it be to give her back?*—Gage gestured toward the house. "Were you waiting long, Tina? I didn't think we were late."

Jenna's mind hiccupped and caught up. Had Gage arranged this meeting behind Leeann's back? Perhaps he'd bribed Tina to come all the way out here. Which didn't seem to make her a very trustworthy person to leave in charge of a young child.

Gage swung open the door and they stepped into a living room that was…ordinary. Timber and tapestry furniture that looked homey rather than imposing. A stone fireplace built into the far tongue-and-groove wall. A quaint grandfather clock stood ticking in one corner. Scattered rugs on the flagstone floor…a vase of daisies on the table…

She loved it!

Gage curled a knuckle around her cheek. "I think you should hold your niece."

Jenna nodded fiercely, but as soon as Tina laid a sleeping Meg in her aunt's arms, the thrill of this huge surprise twirled around and hit Jenna high in the stomach.

Her throat felt so thick, she couldn't swallow. Only smile.

"She's so beautiful."

Gage stood close beside her, looking down, too. That knuckle touched Meg's cheek. Her little mouth pouted and sucked in and out, as if she were having a dream about dinner.

Gage grunted—a satisfied sound. "She certainly is cute."

"She is, indeed. And now I'll leave you both alone to enjoy her."

Tina's words snapped Jenna back. Alone? "Where are you going?"

Amy had been gone almost a month. What if Meg didn't recognize her face and cried? The very thought ripped the heart from Jenna's chest, but how could she deny the possibility? She'd rather be in pain herself than see Meg upset.

Gage walked down a hallway. "There's a sunroom down here, Tina, with magazines and cable. An Internet connection too, if you're interested."

Jenna's locked muscles relaxed. Meg's nanny wouldn't be too far away then.

Tina tapped the tote bag slung over her shoulder. "I have a book, thank you." She stepped closer to Jenna. "She'll most likely be uncertain when she wakes to find a…" Her brow pinched. "A different face."

She had only confirmed what Jenna already knew. Leeann, and Tina, had become the people the baby knew and relied upon now.

Jenna gazed down at Meg, so warm and snug in her arms. She nodded. "If she gets upset, I'll have Gage get you."

Tina's smile was appreciative. "Her bag with a written routine is in the front seat of the car."

"I'll get that," Gage offered, returning from having opened a door at the end of that hall. "Make yourself comfortable, Tina. There's a kitchenette in there, too."

Tina had no sooner closed the door behind her than Meg began to stir. Jenna's knees went weak. *Please don't cry, little girl. Please remember me.*

But she settled back to sleep again, curling toward Jenna's breast.

"Surprised?"

Jenna suppressed a laugh. "That's a huge understatement. How did you arrange it?" Her gut pitched. "What will Leeann say?"

"Leeann knows. I contacted her when we arrived back from New Zealand and told her how eager I was to discuss Darley Realty, that I should still be able to make the date we'd arranged for the meeting, but could we get in a nice long visit with Meg beforehand."

Jenna could barely believe her ears. He didn't pull any punches. "And she said yes?"

"Meg is ours until tomorrow lunchtime. It's in writing, so Leeann can't change her story later."

"And Tina?"

His lips twitched. "I have a feeling Tina will enjoy the break—not from Meg but from Leeann. She's staying overnight, too. There's a guest bedroom in that wing."

Slowly waking, Meg stretched an arm and squeaked. Jenna's body tensed. "I've never looked after a baby before."

He chuckled. "Better get used to it."

As the baby moved against Jenna, a sensation of real hope seeped through her. "You really think we have a chance?"

His expression hardened almost imperceptibly. "I normally get what I want, Jenna. I want this for you."

Her eyes misted over; she wanted to ask what else he wanted. But she was scared of the reply. Scared he wouldn't confirm that his needs for the future included them.

Meg blew a bubble and dragged open her eyes. Her lashes swept down again, her flawless brow pinched, then she blinked her eyes fully open.

Jenna held her breath and gently murmured, "Hello, sweetie."

Meg's gaze grew more intense, the corners of her mouth quaked, then she blinked twice more and slowly, slowly smiled.

Jenna choked on a teary laugh.

Gage whispered beside her. "I'm hungry when I wake up. Should we feed her now?"

Jenna carefully sloped the baby up in her arm as Meg seemed to focus more on her. In fact, wouldn't take her eyes off her. "Let's get her bag. Tina mentioned a routine." Guilt knotted in her stomach. "I should have done more research on infants. I just hadn't expected…"

She took in Meg again and relaxed a notch as the warm stir of instinct seemed to take over. "I think a diaper change would be a good idea."

With long strides, Gage headed for the door. "Diapers coming up."

Five minutes later they were in the nursery, Meg on the changing table, Gage handing over the wipes. He hung further back than Jenna thought entirely necessary.

She hid a grin. "Powder, please."

Meg blew more bubbles, clenched her tiny fist and kicked her heels.

Gage's expression, by contrast, was intense. He rummaged around the baby bag then slapped the powder bottle in Jenna's open palm. "Powder."

Her grin became a laugh. "This isn't an operation."

"Coulda fooled me." Gage gingerly tied the plastic bag that contained the soiled diaper.

Jenna applied the powder then set the new diaper under the baby's bottom. She fixed the tabs, grateful for this day, for Gage's help and his resilience.

She stole a quick glance at him. "I'm proud of you."

He grunted. "Me? Why?"

"I don't know a lot of men who'd be brave enough to tackle that right off the bat." She eyed the diaper bag.

He cocked a brow and held the bag up by one tie. "To be fair to the rest of my gender, it does take courage."

His lopsided grin wrapped around her heart—and squeezed. This exchange was feeling way too comfortable. Too dangerous. *Save that heart of yours, Jenna, and don't get used to it.*

She slipped Meg's bloomers back on then eased her up into her arms. Oh, it felt so good!

She faced Gage. "Want to have a nurse?"

Gage's easy smile shifted enough for a frown line to form between his brows. He ran a hand over Meg's crown. "This is your time. I'm here to assist."

Jenna didn't let her hurt show. After all, what did she expect? If—correction, *when*—the guardianship situation was settled and she and Meg were together without any doubt of separation, Gage would get on with his life. He'd made it clear he didn't want the full-time commitment that went with kids. So it was better that he was wise enough not to get too close now.

Meg grabbed Jenna's finger, her beautiful face glowing as if she truly knew her auntie. Or perhaps it was the memory of her wonderful mother's face that Meg was reacting to.

Jenna bit her inside cheek.

No tears today. This was "happy" time.

"Why don't we get a blanket and sit under a tree," Gage suggested. "She might enjoy the scenery. I read somewhere that babies like colors."

Smiling up at her husband, Jenna walked with him out the door. "I think you're right."

They spent the afternoon talking to the baby, feeding the baby, burping then singing to the baby. After six hours, Jenna was bushed. So was Meg.

Tina popped her head out from her room as Jenna was preparing to put Meg down. "Everything going well?"

Gage was folding the picnic blanket. "Absolutely.

Thanks, Tina." Whistling, he continued on to the laundry room, not a usual occurrence in a billionaire's day.

Tina joined Jenna and cooed at Meg. "She had a bath before our drive. We'll give her another in the morning." She straightened and smiled at Jenna. "Need any help putting her down?"

Jenna hadn't been sure of Tina when they'd first met, and she'd jumped to the wrong conclusions about possible bribes and lack of responsibility when she'd seen her earlier today. But now Jenna got the best feeling that she and Tina would know and like each other for a long time to come.

She smiled. "I'd like to try to put her down myself. I'll call if I need help."

Tina nodded then pressed a kiss to Meg's brow. Eyes heavy, the baby yawned. "She's ready for a night's sleep. Lay her in the cot, sing her a lullaby. She'll fuss but nod off quickly."

Twenty minutes later, she and Gage stood in the nursery with the nightlight casting slow spinning stars over the ceiling and walls. Meg was still in Jenna's arms, and more than a little fussy. She did *not* want to go down. For the first time all afternoon, Jenna felt her insecurities taking over.

She murmured as she gently rubbed Meg's back. "It's okay, sweetie. Aunt Jenna's here."

Nearby, Gage scrubbed his jaw. "She needs another bottle."

"She's just a little out of sorts in a new environment. I'll put her down again." Surely she'd nod off this time.

But five minutes later, Meg had worked up a steady cry. Her face was red and her poor little mouth was trembling. Jenna had sung and sung, and held her wee hand, while Gage paced up a storm in the background.

He shoveled a hand through his hair and joined her by the cot. "I'll get Tina."

At her wits' end, Jenna was about to give in and agree when a thought struck her. "Let me try something first."

She scooped a whimpering Meg up and handed her to Gage, who reacted by standing stock-still. His voice cracked. "What do you want me to do with her?"

"Hold her a minute."

Jenna straightened the cot blanket then headed for the nightlight while Meg hiccupped and shuddered out a breath. With fumbling fingers, Jenna managed to find the switch and stop the stars from spinning.

She pivoted back to Gage. "Maybe there was too much stimulation—"

Her words trailed off. Just like that, Meg's eyes had shut. No crying. No movement. Her mouth was parted and, free from her rug, her little arm hung over Gage's.

Gage's eyes were round with amazement. He shrugged. "What did I do?"

Jenna wanted to laugh out loud. She threw up her arms. "I have no idea."

But in truth, maybe she did. Despite their past, she always felt safest when she was bundled in Gage's arms. Why should Meg feel any different?

They stood there, simply enjoying watching her sleep. Her cheeks were pink and chubby, a tiny dimple in her chin. Thank heaven she was healthy.

Jenna finally whispered, "Do you want to ease her down onto the mattress?"

"I need to hold her a bit longer. Just to be sure."

Jenna kept her eyes on Gage, who kept his eyes on Meg.

She smiled. "I think you're right."

Two hours later, Gage sat in the nursery's comfortable corner lounge, Meg still in his arms. He'd fallen asleep not long after Meg. He'd been up since three that morning; seemed it had been a tiring day all around.

Legs drawn up, chin resting on her knees, Jenna hugged her shins and watched from the cushioned window seat. She didn't want Meg to fall from Gage's arms. But in her heart Jenna knew that wasn't possible. The baby looked as if she belonged there and perhaps in slumber Meg felt it, too.

Jenna was still drinking in the picture when Gage awoke. His chest inflated then, eyes shooting open, he moved to sit up straight. Immediately he remembered the baby and gingerly settled back down. He gazed at Meg for a long moment before he searched the room.

Feeling all syrupy and warm, Jenna eased up and stretched her back. "I think we can put her down now," she whispered.

Gage took a few moments to push to his feet. Jenna smoothed the sheets then stood back as Gage lowered the baby. Meg didn't move a muscle.

Jenna held her breath as a bone-chilling thought hit her. "Is she breathing?"

Gage's hand zipped down to hover near her nose then drew back. "Definitely breathing."

He threaded an arm around her waist and Jenna leaned in. So warm and big.

"Thank you."

He pulled her close. "My pleasure. Which reminds

me…" He angled her around, set his forehead against hers then stole the softest kiss. "Bed for the grown-ups sounds like a good idea."

"A very good idea," she murmured against his lips.

He watched over Meg while she showered. Then she took the watch while he cleaned up. When they finally climbed into bed in the room connected to the nursery, they didn't sleep, didn't make love. Rather they both lay there, staring at the ceiling.

"Do you think she'll wake through the night?" Jenna asked.

Gage crooked an arm to cup a palm under his head. "If she does, we'll hear her."

Of course, he was right. There was nothing to worry about. Nothing at all.

In the dark, Gage rolled over to face her. She could distinguish the outline of his shoulder and the white of his smile in the shadows. "You suit being a mother."

"You suit being a dad."

She felt him stiffen and a shrinking head-tingling sensation dropped through her.

It had slipped out. She knew very well Gage's position. He didn't want to be a father. This situation was temporary…a ruse with good sex thrown in. It was never meant to be, and obviously never *would* be anything else.

Following an interminable silence, he rolled onto his back. "We should get some sleep."

But Jenna lay awake for what seemed like hours. And she could tell by his breathing that Gage did the same—staring at the ceiling and wondering, just like her.

Ten

Jenna woke with a start.

Something—a baby—was squealing.

In a single heartbeat, the day and night before flashed into her brain.

Meg! Something was wrong.

In her pink singlet and matching shorts, she sprang out of bed, tripping over herself to get to the nursery. When she flew in the room, Gage was already there, lifting her niece out of the cot. The squealing, Jenna realized, was a sound of pure delight. With care, Gage swung the baby round on his arm so she sat perched facing Jenna, baby blues wide and twinkling.

Slumping with relief, Jenna pushed her palm against her pounding heart. Then she marched over and spoke softly to Meg. "You scared me, baby."

"It's after seven." Gage jiggled Meg and she giggled. "We've got ourselves a sleeper."

Jenna's heartbeat kicked. He'd never looked more handsome—dark hair mussed, masculine chest bared, his open expression devoid of any thought other than the tiny human being relying on him at this moment. He was so capable. So strong.

To her soul Jenna knew that from this point on, Gage would be the only man to ever kiss or touch her. She'd believed that before they'd met again; now, having given him her virginity, she was certain of it. She was just as sure about herself and Meg needing to be together.

A question formed in her mind before she could tamp it down.

How could he *not* change his mind about family now that he'd been with Meg, even if it had only been for a single day? She hadn't believed it was possible, but after this time spent together, she was even more hooked than before. She only wished now it could be the three of them—not pretending, but for real.

Gage's easy expression shifted as if he realized how he must look. Like a family man. Everything he didn't want long term.

A muscle beat in his jaw as he offered her the baby.

Jenna thought of making some excuse for him to hold her longer and reinforce in his mind how right this baby must feel in his arms. But that wouldn't be fair. All she'd prayed for was an answer to her problem, and hopefully her prayer would be answered by the intervention of the most unlikely person. She must be happy with the solution and not hold out for another miracle.

Gage hadn't said or done anything to indicate that

he'd changed his mind. When this was over, he would leave, and he'd take her heart with him. But she would try not to mourn—not this time. That wouldn't be fair on anyone, including Meg.

She took the baby and the day progressed. First a change, then a breakfast bottle, then a bath. Gage stood a little closer than he had the day before, dribbling the washcloth over Meg's round little tummy, laughing when Meg splashed and chirped and squealed.

Over a game of "clap hands," Gage took a video using his cell phone, as well as several photos, some with the baby alone, then with Tina. Finally Tina took a few of the three of them together—Jenna, Gage and Meg. Tina said she'd like a copy.

At eleven o'clock it was time to leave. Time for breaking hearts.

Outside, while Gage locked up and Tina pulled her car around, Jenna held the baby, her lips pressed to Meg's satin-soft brow. Her mind wouldn't work, refusing to go forward and contemplate the next few minutes. She closed her eyes as tears leaked from the corners. Her chest felt as if it had caved in and her spirit had been crushed beneath the weight.

This is where you belong. How can I let you go again? If I don't get you back, how will I bear it?

She simply had to win guardianship. Gage's plan— this pretend marriage—had to work.

"Jenna, it's time."

She needed every ounce of willpower to open her eyes and meet his gaze. Gage's expression was almost impassive, as if he'd turned off his feelings. But when his nostrils flared the barest amount, she was certain this was hard for him, as well.

Because he didn't want to see Jenna hurt? Or because he was hurting too?

Gage put out his hands, palms up. "I'll buckle her in."

Jenna held her breath, felt her eyes go wide, and told herself to just do it.

When the baby left her arms, the air in Jenna's lungs evaporated. It felt as if her soul had been ripped away.

Tina appeared beside her. "I'll take good care of her until next time."

Jenna nodded even as her heart broke open like an empty shell. Yes, there would be a *next time* and maybe soon an *all the time*. She had to stay focused on that or how would she make it through these coming days?

Still, when Tina's car drove off down the crushed pebbled drive, Jenna felt her heart go, too.

Gage wrapped his arms around her, rocking her gently with his chin resting on her crown. "Be brave a while longer."

She swallowed against the anguish stinging her eyes and nose. Then she filled her lungs deeply and looked up into those thoughtful pale gray eyes.

"When this is over," Jenna said, "and Meg's home to stay, we're going to have the biggest damn party ever thrown."

The smile almost reached his eyes.

He tucked her head back under his chin. "You bet we will."

Sitting out on the penthouse's main balcony four days later, Jenna ran her gaze over Sydney's sparkling cityscape and sighed. Would that big party ever be thrown, or was she still just kidding herself?

Of course, nothing could go forward with Meg until after Gage's meeting with Leeann at the end of the week. Patience was needed as well as trust in her husband's judgment. Still, the clawing anticipation of the final outcome kept dragging her down. She was only grateful that, despite his own worries, Gage seemed to be doing his utmost to keep her spirits high.

Gage joined her on the balcony, a carafe of juice in hand to go with lunch. Halfway into his rattan chair, his cell phone sounded. Growling, he set the carafe down heavily enough for the orange juice to splash on the cloth.

Jenna pressed her lips together. Normally he was so cool—effortlessly in charge—yet lately the more his phone rang or that fax beeped, the more edgy he became. The Meg dilemma might be Jenna's sole upset, but she couldn't forget that Gage was an important man with a load of responsibilities, which she couldn't begin to imagine.

She'd heard Dubai mentioned several times and more than wondered whether his negotiations with the hotel consortium he'd spoken of briefly were facing major problems. On numerous occasions after taking a call, he would disappear inside his master suite for an hour at a time. Sometimes she'd hear him yelling. Now that phone was pressed to his ear again.

She gazed down at her meal. She'd be finishing her shelled lobster alone. Or what she could of it. Although it looked better than delicious, she had little appetite these days.

Concentrating on the call, Gage's brow creased. "Yes, I see." An eyebrow flexed. "Is that right?" A smile spread across his face. "That's marvelous. See you then."

Jenna pushed balsamic-dressed lettuce around her plate. "Good news?" *For a change?*

Gage swept up the carafe and filled her glass then his own. "That was my lawyer."

Jenna's ears pricked. "Lance?"

Was he calling about their petition for guardianship? Perhaps there'd been an early date set, or a judge assigned who might be sympathetic toward their case.

"My contractual lawyer, Jenna, not personal."

Hope fading, she set her fork down. "Oh."

"Not just *oh*. He spoke with Darley Realty's financial controller. Mr. Arnold asked that the preliminary documentation be put in order in the event of a buyout going through."

"But we already know Leeann wants you to buy the company. It's no good to her in the state it's in. Anything you offer would be a boon. That doesn't mean at this stage that she's willing to give up Meg for a deal."

His mouth slanted with a mysterious grin. "It tells me she's seriously thinking about it. The afternoon we arrived back from our day in the country with Meg, I took the liberty of pushing our hand."

Jenna stopped breathing. "Go on."

"I made her a verbal offer, an obscene amount of money if she signed two sets of documents. One as the vendor for Darley Realty, the other, a legally binding statement that specifies you and me as the best guardians for Meg. It states all the reasons we've put forward in our petition, and will give permission between the two parties for us to take Meg home immediately."

Jenna's heart hammered a wonderful staccato

against her ribs. The sky looked suddenly bluer. Even the sun felt warmer on her skin. "We won't have to go to court?"

"We'll still have a judge sanction the decision. Clearly, if the testamentary guardian relinquishes responsibility to a blood relative—the deceased's own twin—there'll be no objection. At the end of the day the court wants the best for the child." He grinned. "You're the best."

She jumped out of her chair and threw her arms around his neck. "I can't believe it! Maybe you should pinch me."

"The offer is on the table until the day of our meeting. The following day the offer will be halved. The next day I'll tell Leeann to shove the business and we'll win Meg back through the courts."

Jenna shivered. *Ruthless man.* "I'm glad you're on my side."

He drew her down onto his lap. "So am I."

She loved him. It was that simple. She always had and always would. The rebel she'd once known had a good heart, even if it were an incredibly lonely and, in some ways, damaged one. But she wouldn't let her mind wander to places where it might get lost. If she tried to cling to dreams she couldn't hold, she might slip and fall again into that deep dark hole—the one she'd barely been able to claw back out from when he'd left her the last time.

But she had him here and now. For as long as it lasted, she wouldn't waste a minute, not a second. Every tick of the clock was precious, another memory to live on and last for the rest of her life.

She grazed a fingertip over his bottom lip then

back again. "Perhaps we should continue our cele-
bration inside."

His fingers threaded up through her hair and brought
her head down to his.

He kissed her until she couldn't fathom which way
was up and then, as if she weighed no more than a bag
full of feathers, he rose to his feet with her slung in his
arms. "It just so happens I have a bottle of vintage Bol-
linger chilling as we speak."

"What? No party balloons?"

He headed for the bedroom. "Not the kind you're
thinking."

They didn't emerge from the bedroom until much
later, and only to order in food—club sandwiches, extra
fries, and lemon meringue pie with two giant bowls of
whipped cream.

Enjoying a sit-down picnic on the living room rug,
Gage leant back on one arm, swallowed a mouthful of
pie and chuckled.

Jenna's spoon stopped midway to her mouth.
"What's funny?"

"A dollop of cream's hanging from your chin."

Jenna brushed her face, felt the cream smear then
saw it on her hand.

"I don't have any bibs." He licked his spoon, front
then back. "But I'd be happy to feed you, if that'd
help."

She grinned. *Smart aleck.*

"You're so sweet," she gushed. "But if one of us
needs a bib…" She scooped up a finger full of pie and
wiped it down his chest. "I think it might be you."

When he met her gaze again, a look of bedevilment

shone in his eyes. "You shouldn't have done that, Jenna. There's an awful lot of cream and meringue here."

He dropped his spoon and collected his bowl with two hands.

Almost repentant, Jenna shrank back. "You wouldn't dare."

His white teeth flashed. "Dare is my middle name."

Jenna shrieked when cream splattered on her shoulder, and again when it hit the rug near her leg. When he fired at her nose, she picked up her own bowl and decided to even the score.

By the time the food fight had lost momentum, pie was pretty much everywhere—arms, legs and an assortment of places in between. As the victor, Gage pinned Jenna down and proceeded to finish his dessert, which meant savoring skin-warmed cream for him and unparalleled pleasure for her.

Finally, feeling satisfied but sticky all over, Jenna shimmied out from beneath him.

He grabbed her arm as she rose to leave. "We're not finished yet."

"I ate, I came, I conquered. Now I need a shower."

"I'm not sure that's how it goes, however," he rubbed a palm over his cream-smeared chest, "I follow your drift."

The moment he jumped up, that blasted fax beeped again. His expression clouded over to almost black; he didn't even think to excuse himself before he strode across to retrieve the message.

Jenna's hands fisted at her sides. *For pity's sake.* Just for once, couldn't they leave him alone? Guess she'd see him later—much later.

She entered her room remembering his comment the

day they'd met again—the remark that had established from the get-go that he wasn't a man meant for family. *A child needs a stable home life.* He was right, of course. Any woman who was genuinely married to Gage would need to be endlessly understanding of his commitments, particularly if she had a child begging for her father's severely limited time.

Thinking of Meg again, Jenna entered her private bathroom, which was huge and close to decadent—all shiny green marble and gold-rimmed mirrors. The shower recess was floor-to-ceiling glass on three sides, spacious enough to house hanging baskets of ferns and an assortment of potted palms. Showering was like bathing beneath a secluded waterfall in the jungle.

She adjusted the temperature on the nearest of two nozzles and, stepping under, let the warm, soft spray wash her stickiness away. Her head was back, her hair hanging and wet, when she heard a soft echoing click. She blinked beyond the water running down her face. Gage's long, strong legs stepped past a crow's-nest fern, into the center of the recess.

Hard, hot and naked, he released the second nozzle and its hose from the wall. He found the right temperature and those broad shoulders rotated toward her. "When I make a mess, I clean it up…thoroughly."

While her body tingled at his deep commanding tone, he took both her hands in one of his then waved the spray back and forth over her fingers, her open palms, the sensitive skin of her inner wrists. She could barely believe he'd squared away whatever problem that fax had delivered and was with her again so soon. But she wouldn't look a gift horse in the mouth.

Every minute…every second…

Finished with her hands, he lifted her fingers and kissed each individual gnawed-down tip. So simple an act yet already she was simmering.

She was about to lace her arms around his neck when he frowned. "My job's not finished. Turn around, hands on the wall."

She blinked. "Am I under arrest?"

"Depends on how well you follow orders."

A delicious shiver raced over her skin. Smiling, she stroked his chin and turned around.

The water flowed back and forth on her shoulder blades, then lower against her back as his thumb pressed skilful circles over tiny hidden knots. As each tension point loosened, her arousal wound tighter, and the flames in her belly leapt high.

His massage reached her hip, and her one ticklish spot. Gasping, she swept back around. "Okay. I'm clean now."

His smile was amusement studded with sin. "You want me to stop?"

"I wish you'd never stop."

They both seemed to stop breathing.

Was she sorry she'd said it? Because she meant every word. What they were enjoying now couldn't last, and yet…if she could make another wish she would ask that they be married in more than name only. She knew it was madness and yet, little by little she was convincing herself that long term wasn't impossible.

As she trembled with anticipation and beating physical need, his eyes narrowed as if he were making a choice. Then his gaze roamed her face, the nozzle hit the floor and his knees bent to bracket the outside of hers.

Noses touching, he cupped her bottom and slowly drew her up so her breasts grazed over the ruts of his stomach then the matted steel of his chest. When her legs scissored around his hips, keeping his eyes on her mouth, he began to shift her weight—right then left, gently up and down. She slipped slightly and, for stability's sake, he pressed her carefully back against the wall.

"Is that too cold?"

She drove her hands through his hair. "What do you think?"

When at last he entered her, an incredible wave of heat and passion rolled all the way through her. It was like a gathering storm, tossing all her emotions together, whipping them high, sending them clashing against one another in a maelstrom of feverish joy. With his mouth on her neck, she clutched onto his shoulders and whispered the words in her mind…

I love you. I love you. I always, always will.

As if those thoughts had cast a spell, the throbbing inside her intensified and spiraled out of control. Unable to hold back, she plunged off the precipice into a glorious white-hot pit; holding her tight, Gage came, too.

While she gave herself over to the irresistible magic, he murmured her name in that deep throaty voice—the same tone she knew so well and adored. And yet…

Something was different.

They'd made love countless times but tonight his embrace felt surer, his words sounded truer. And the feeling…?

As his face buried into her shoulder, Jenna remembered the water raining down around them and the fact that they'd both forgotten protection. Gage didn't seem aware of it even now.

She chewed her lip.

Was it possible—even subconsciously—that Gage was learning to swim?

Eleven

Gage rapped his knuckles against his trouser thigh then straightened his royal blue tie and gold cuff links. For the first time in a decade of top-level business negotiations, *damn it all,* he was nervous.

"Don't worry," he told Jenna, who sat before him in Darley Realty's opulent reception lounge. "This'll all be over in a few minutes."

They'd arrived at these offices precisely on time for their long-awaited appointment with Leeann and her financial controller. His documents had been delivered by courier the day before. All that remained was to get her signature on the dotted lines. Simple.

That woman's self-centered greed would surely reign supreme. He had no doubt Leeann would take the deal—a bundle of money in exchange for Darley Realty and little Meg.

Soon his biggest debt would be repaid.

Soon this all would be over.

He ignored the sharp jab in his gut and tugged on his cuff links again. "After she signs, we'll go straight to collect Meg."

A ragged thumbnail left Jenna's mouth. "I'm glad you're confident. The superstitious part of me doesn't want to jinx today by being too sure."

"Then I'll be sure for us both."

And when Meg was safely back in Jenna's care, he needed to jump on his jet and shoot over to Dubai. Nick had flown over to work the problems through, only to discover that the head honchos wouldn't deal with anyone but Gage Cameron himself. Nick had managed to placate the ruffled feathers, but the fabric of this deal was held together now by the barest of threads. If he didn't get there in the next thirty-six hours, he might as well kiss that billion dollars goodbye. The players had been new to him; this deal had always been somewhat of a gamble, but his gambles always paid off. This would *not* be his first failure. Damned if it would.

When his gaze and thoughts landed back on Jenna, he bit down against a pang of longing. He'd known this would end. More importantly, he'd made certain Jenna had known it too. There was no room for regrets because that only left room for more hurt. He cared too deeply for Jenna to leave her hanging, tied up over someone who couldn't be a partner to what she needed more than air. Her family. Or what remained of it. Better for him to make as clean a break as possible.

Better to be safe. If she knew his deeper reasons, she'd agree.

He cast a look over one shoulder at the doors that would take him to the boardroom. "Sure you don't want to come in?" She'd most likely enjoy watching Leeann sweat. Neither of them owed that woman any favors.

Jenna set her hands in the lap of her white linen suit. "I'll wait here. Hurry back."

When he was ushered in the boardroom moments later, Gage felt his blood pressure rise. What game were they playing? Why the delay?

A squat man in an ill-fitting suit stood at the far end of a gleaming boardroom table. Smiling, he tipped his balding head at Gage. "Mr. Cameron."

"Mr. Arnold." He flung a glance around the empty room. "If Mrs. Darley is held up, I can give her five minutes' grace. I have a full day ahead."

A huge understatement.

"Mrs. Darley regrets she is unable to attend this morning's meeting. She's away on urgent business. Furthermore she apologizes for wasting your time in coming here this morning."

An arctic chill swept up Gage's spine but years of experience and natural acumen meant the flash of doubt didn't show on his face.

"You should remind Mrs. Darley that my current offer is valid only until midnight. This is hardly a time to bluff."

Moving forward, Mr. Arnold smoothed down his comb over. "No games, Mr. Cameron. There's been a rather startling turn of events with regard to Darley Realty and its position. There's also another matter Mrs. Darley wishes for me to discuss with you. It's regarding the child."

* * *

When Gage walked back into that reception area, he'd never been more rattled in his life bar once. Not because he'd failed to secure a business deal. Hell, that had nothing to do with the ice freezing the blood in his veins. Today he'd been bargaining in flesh and blood and he'd been arrogant enough to believe he would win.

How could he tell Jenna?

When he caught sight of her, she bounced to her feet, but he was certain his eyes told her everything she needed to know. Where was that poker face now?

Jenna froze. Then the life went from her face, her shoulders sagged and she swayed. He hurried to catch her.

She felt boneless in his arms, and she'd lost all her color. Even her lips had turned white.

"She's keeping Meg, isn't she?" she croaked.

His answer was shards of glass pushed up his throat. "Something's come up. Something I didn't expect."

Hell's fire, he should've been more thorough, should've acted sooner. A week earlier and this could've been wrapped up. Now they would need to rely on a judge.

"We won't talk here." He secured her waist and half carried her past the curious receptionist toward the sliding-glass doors.

In the car, he threw his jacket in the back, dragged loose his tie and, arms straight out, set his hands on the wheel. He didn't start the engine.

"That worthless piece of land in Western Australia," he explained, "apparently isn't so worthless. Global demands for iron ore have never been higher. An overseas conglomerate, which is leasing the iron ore holdings on a neighboring concern, has offered a small fortune to buy your father's land."

She shook her head. "Whatever for? I remember Amy saying there were no mineral deposits to speak of."

"She was right. The iron ore deposits are negligible compared to other pockets in W.A. It's the locality this company is interested in tying up. They want to utilize the property's coastline, and clear passage to it, in order to develop their own shipping port and maximize export capabilities. It seems to be the big thing these days."

Comprehension dawned in her eyes. "So she gets her small fortune and also keeps Meg."

He swallowed the nauseous feeling creeping up the back of his throat. "We won't waste any more time there. Now we need to focus our energies on impressing that judge."

Although it hammered at his brain, he wouldn't think about what he could or couldn't do about the Dubai blowout now. Just as he refused to think about the possibility of them losing in court. It only made sense that Meg should be with them—

He lost his breath.

Not with *them*. With Jenna.

Damn it, he meant *Jenna*.

He clamped his eyes shut and groaned. He had no idea this would hurt so much. All he could see in his mind's eye besides Jenna's tears was baby Meg's beaming little face. The way she'd looked and felt in his arms when she slept. And that was dangerous. He had no right to that kind of warmth.

His hands wrung the wheel. "Want to hear the kicker?"

Staring dazedly ahead, she half nodded.

"Leeann went to the police," he said. "She filed a restraining order against you."

Her face twisted. "What in heaven's name for?"

"Her man Arnold cited an alleged incident at our country home the day Meg visited."

"She's saying I hurt *Meg?*" Jenna spat out a curse. "That's ridiculous. Tina was there. She'll substantiate our—"

"Tina's going to testify against you."

A puff of air left her mouth as if she'd been kicked in the stomach. "I liked Tina. I *trusted* her." Her eyes widened, clouding with worry. "Those two women are going to bring Meg up. Liars and manipulators. What hope does she have?"

Gage knew firsthand how a person's sense of self-worth could suffer as a result of bad parenting. When a kid was old enough to understand the dynamics, the damage was already done. If a person were strong enough—if he had a leg up—he might be able to lift himself out of the bog. But in his experience there would always be something left behind…something missing. Whenever he got too close, that missing part—the slice of his soul that needed its distance—would rattle its cage and howl to be free.

That's when people got hurt.

Some even died.

Jenna's insulted tone brought him back. "What exactly is she accusing me of?"

His hands dropped from the wheel. "Arnold wouldn't expand on that. But he did ramble on about some other cock-and-bull tale—your prior dependency on prescribed drugs, as well as a history of depression. We'll have no problem refuting that in court. They'll only make fools of themselves without any evidence."

"It's true."

She caught him off-guard and he shot her a look. "What's true?"

Jenna's face was expressionless as if she'd given up hope. "When you left without a word I was so down I literally couldn't get out of bed. Amy was away, so Dad asked Leeann to take me to her GP. The doctor explained about stress and brain chemicals and compromised function. He said I might need some help to get back on my feet." Her chest rose and fell on a worn-down sigh. "Antidepressants didn't make the pain go away, but they helped me to keep going. Although I knew it was nothing to be ashamed of, Leeann took pleasure in mentioning it whenever she could until my father told her to stop."

Gage managed to clamp shut his hanging jaw. *My God. I did that to you.*

Didn't matter that he'd been young and thought he'd done the right thing—leaving Jenna before he could get her in trouble, unlike his father who'd screwed up Gage's mother's life by getting her pregnant at seventeen. And, yes, he'd had to escape Leeann's accusations; attempted rape was a serious offence. But if he'd been man enough, he would have found a different way. Right?

Growling, he shook his head at his lap.

Wrong. This revelation about Jenna's illness after he'd left merely proved his point. Fact was that he burned people he got close to…burned them bad.

Gage glanced over at Jenna. She was plowing through her handbag like a dog after a bone.

"I'm going to call Leeann and tell her exactly what I think," she ground out. "If she won't talk to me, I'll go over there and—"

"No, you won't." He took the phone from her.

Her eyes flashed, then she snatched it back and held it from him. Her voice shook and so did her hand. "Don't try to stop me."

For God's sake! "Leeann isn't even in the *state*."

Hearing his voice rise, he tamped down the barrage of emotions hurtling through his overloaded system and set his fraying nerves on a more even keel.

"Leave this to me, Jenna. I'll do whatever it takes to make things right."

The tears brimming in her eyes fell down her cheeks. "How? You know what will happen. In court her attorney will exaggerate those few months I took medication. They'll say I won't make a fit mother. Gage, I need to do something *now*. That baby needs me. *I* need her."

Damn it. "So do I!"

The mind-numbing realization fell upon him like a collapsing building, but he shoved the rubble away. Hell, he'd only met the child twice. He'd held her, played with her. Admittedly some kind of connection had been made, but his goal had always been to have any connection live on through Jenna.

That baby deserved someone a whole lot better than him.

Jenna was gaping at him. Before she could ask, he apologized. "Forgive me. I shouldn't have…shouldn't have raised my voice."

Her tone was calmer but still urgent. "I need to speak with Tina. Maybe if we offered her money, or found out why she's willing to lie…"

He concentrated, his mind hopscotching to various possibilities and solutions. If there was a way, he'd damn well find it.

He fired the engine and threw it into reverse.

As the car veered, Jenna tossed from one side of her seat to the other. She reached for the seat belt. "Where are we going?"

He stepped on the gas and shot out onto the street. "To see justice done."

Twelve

When the Maserati screeched to a stop outside the property Leeann had moved back into with Meg, and Jenna had once called home, Gage swung open his door.

With one leg out, he said over his shoulder, "Wait here."

Her door was already open. "No way!"

His hot hand snared her arm like a bear trap. "There's a restraining order pending against you. Don't make matters worse."

Jenna tensed. Gage had gone above and beyond the call of duty to try to secure guardianship of Meg. Marrying her, buying her that gorgeous house in the country, he'd even been willing to spend an obscene amount acquiring Darley Realty as an exchange tactic. But she couldn't and *wouldn't* sit back any longer.

She laid her hand over his. "I appreciate everything you've done, but I need to be more than a bystander now. This was my father's house. This is my niece. It's my battle. I need to face Tina, woman to woman, and see if it's not too late to somehow save this situation."

A muscle in his jaw flexed twice before he blinked and slowly released her arm. He shook his head as if to clear it. "I guess this whole guardianship thing has gotten under my skin."

Jenna's smile was wry.

What was the phrase he'd used when all this had started? *Let the games begin.* But this had turned into far more than a game for Gage. He truly cared about Meg and with whom she'd live. He'd been visibly shaken when he'd found out his exchange plan had failed. Later in the car he'd confessed that he'd needed Meg too.

The words burned on her tongue. *I love you. I think you love me, too.* With every passing day, it seemed more and more right that they should stay together— not in a mock marriage but as a real family. A family of three who loved one another, who were there every day and every night to support and to care.

People *did* change when they had a good enough reason. She'd come home, hadn't she?

Why couldn't he?

Gage helped her out of the car then fanned open one side of the iron gates. Ears pricked high, Shadow loped down the long drive. Gage hadn't shut the gate before Shadow jumped up in welcome. After slobbering over Jenna's hand, he sped off into the trees.

Gage brushed down his trousers. "At least someone's happy to see us."

Jenna's smile faded as she surveyed the property and an eerie sensation crept up each vertebra. Leeann had never liked the man her father employed to maintain the grounds. She must have let him go because the lawn was unkempt, the garden lacked water, but the trees unsettled her the most. They seemed to be peering down, judging or, perhaps, pleading with her somehow.

Why did you leave? Why didn't you come home sooner?

Jenna shuddered. No matter what transpired today, she would not return to this place. In a way she was glad her father hadn't left her this house. She didn't need it to remember her family. They would always live on in her heart.

Jenna's adrenaline was pumping by the time they reached the double front doors. Gage grabbed the brass knocker and let it fall three times. After a long tense moment, he tried again then took a few steps back to peer up at the second story.

He shaded his eyes. "Doesn't appear to be anyone home."

She tried to distinguish any movement beyond a heavy drawn curtain. "Tina could be hiding."

"Or she could be out."

Joining Gage, she set her hands on her hips. It was hard to believe that Meg's nanny had betrayed them. She'd had her doubts at first, but Tina had seemed sincere about her responsibilities toward Meg, and anyone who knew Leeann would surely see that woman could only love a child as an object, not a person. Leeann was too self-absorbed to put anyone's feelings before her own.

Shadow reappeared with a heavy stick between his

jaws. He wove around Gage, dropped the stick at his feet then corralled Gage closer to the stairs.

Gage ruffled his fur. "Not now, boy."

But Shadow persisted, dropping the stick, running around, picking it up then trotting down the side of the house.

The hair on Jenna's neck stood up and quivered. "He wants us to follow him."

Gage held out his hand. "I just had the same thought."

Shadow trotted off over the lawn toward the hothouse, then to where the pine trees formed a wall that separated this property from the next—from the house where Gage and his mother had once lived. As they passed the foggy walls of the hothouse, Jenna's heart sank. The prize orchids were limp, beyond rescue. Her father would've cried.

Her chest ached when she saw a plant on the hothouse step that she couldn't leave behind a second time. She collected the bonsai and brushed the brittle brown leaves. "Typical of Leeann to dump it out here."

She'd told Gage the story behind the bonsai late one night in bed. Now, as then, he brought her close and pressed a kiss to her temple. "You'll make it well."

She bit down against the ache in her throat. It might be too late for the others but she'd sure as hell save this one.

On the other side of the hedge she heard voices. Gage put his finger to his mouth and they crept closer. Through a hole in the hedge, the same space Gage had crawled through to see Jenna that summer, they saw them…Leeann and a surprise guest.

Leeann's blond hair for once looked disarrayed. She

swept it out of her face as she pleaded with the man. "I've told you, we need to be patient."

Gage whispered to Jenna. "So much for being out of state. Obviously this is one meeting she couldn't avoid. Do you know that man?"

Jenna shook her head. "But I'm betting on cold nights he wears a leather jacket."

Gage nodded at the same time the man smashed his beer bottle onto the cracked concrete drive. Jenna and Leeann both jumped.

"I'm *sick* of waiting." The man's voice was low and desperate. "The authorities are still looking into the crash. They've already come around asking me questions. If they find out I reversed the main rotor belt, I can kiss the next twenty-five years goodbye."

Prickling stars rushed over Jenna's scalp. Her vision grew dark before she blinked back to fully comprehend what she'd just heard.

My God. These two had killed her father. Amy and Brad too.

As bile rose at the back of her throat the name came to her. Barry…? Barry Whitmore. She'd read it in the police accident report. This man had been her father's helicopter mechanic. He did all the maintenance work on the *Squirrel,* Darley Realty's six-seater Eurocopter. It seemed Barry's last job hadn't been about upkeep or repairs, but sabotage.

Barry walked a tight circle, his hand at his brow. Sweat stained his khaki collar and under his arms. "I have nightmares where the police break down my door and haul me away."

Placating him, Leeann stroked his stubbled chin. "If they haven't got any evidence now, they never will.

When a helicopter suffers hydraulic failure doing 120 knots, nothing and no one lives to tell any tales."

He knocked her hand away, self-disgust hanging on his face. "His daughter wasn't supposed to be there. I felt bad enough about the son-in-law. Hell, that baby's got no parents because of us."

The mole on Leeann's left eyebrow lifted. "And now she has a mother who waited a very long time for the privilege."

Jenna fought the impulse to retch. That's how much Leeann wanted Meg—enough to take away the most precious and irreplaceable things in her life. That wasn't love. That was obsession.

Barry rubbed the back of his neck. "I only wanted to get rid of Darley. It was just a matter of time before he found out I was the one you were seeing. If he'd hit you again," his fingers clenched together, "I'd've killed him with my own hands."

Gage clamped a palm over Jenna's mouth before she could blurt anything out. Leeann had played this man. Her father hadn't hit anyone in his life.

While Barry kept ranting and sweating, Leeann examined the hedge as if she'd heard something.

"We need to get out of here," Barry said with a harried glance toward the road. "You've got that story going about your folks in the States." He grabbed her upper arms, desperate love in his eyes. "We could fly out tonight."

She shucked out of his hold. "You know I can't do that. I need to make sure this W.A. deal goes through. Then we'll be able to go anywhere we want for as long as we want."

Movement beside her caught Jenna's eye. Tears of

rage turned into a vengeful smile. Gage had his high-tech cell up and activated. He was recording everything on video! She could've kissed that stupid phone.

Barry wiped a shaky hand down his face. "We committed *murder*, Leeann. Can't you finish this business from somewhere safe, like South America? I did this so we could be together, but not in twin prison cells."

Shadow brushed by Jenna's legs and snarled out a growl. Hearing his growl, Leeann squinted at the hedge and muttered, "Bloody dog." She swooped down on some broken glass and hurled it. "Choke on that, you dumb brute."

Leeann's jaw smacked the dirt when Gage stepped out into plain view.

Barry looked taken aback and raised his fists. "Who the hell are you?"

Gage grinned. "The man who's going to put you both in jail."

Trembling with every conceivable emotion, Jenna joined Gage. "We've recorded your entire conversation, Leeann. All the tragedy you've caused my family…" She swallowed against the raw sting of pain. "At least I'll see you rot in jail for it."

Ready to attack, Barry lunged, but when Gage squared his shoulders and Shadow bared his teeth, the shorter man backed up then scrambled along the side of the weatherboard house.

Wary of the dog, Leeann inched forward, a guilty smile quaking on her lips. "You don't need to go to the police. The baby will be home soon." She held out supplicating hands to Jenna. "Take her. She's yours. And I'll give you everything from the W.A. contract, too."

Moisture shimmered in her coward's eyes. "Just give me a day and I'll be out of your lives for good."

Had Leeann conspired with Barry to kill Raphael because she anticipated divorce and the subsequent dent in her financial security? Or had she planned to do away with all of Jenna's family in order to obtain the baby she'd wanted for so long? Most likely it had been a deadly combination of both. Now Leeann was willing to throw Meg away in exchange for her own neck.

She was almost too pathetic to hate.

Almost.

Gage thumbed in a number and pressed the phone to his ear while Jenna held onto his arm.

"You're right about one thing, Leeann. It is time for you to go away," Jenna lifted her chin, "and never ever come back."

An hour later, Jenna sat on the bench holding a sleeping Meg in her arms. Action was starting to die down all around them—police cars driving off, detectives milling around the house—but the baby was content to dream on.

Gazing down, Jenna was swamped by a deluge of emotions: gratitude that the nightmare was over, that Meg would now be safe with her; sadness knowing her sister and father would be alive today if not for two scum-of-the-earth people; love and respect for the man who'd stood by her during this whole ordeal…the man walking toward her now, his gait long and confident, a supportive smile on his handsome face.

Another man stopped his advance. Gage put his hands in his pockets, ready to answer whatever questions this particular officer asked. Jenna sighed. Just a little longer and they could be together—the three of them. After today's events—their actions and confessions—she couldn't imagine Gage leaving her and Meg now.

Beside Jenna, Tina visibly shuddered. She'd arrived with Meg fifteen minutes ago but her face was still pasty with shock.

"I had my suspicions about Mrs. Darley," Tina said in a daze. "I thought she might be seeing someone. When she canceled her flight to Western Australia at the last minute then told me to take the baby out, I had the worst feeling. But it wasn't my business to pry." She cast a look around. "I can't believe it was as bad as all this. That she was a criminal and planned to take Meg away for good." Her brow wrinkled and she pushed the glasses back on her nose. "You believe that I had no idea about that restraining order, don't you? I could see how much you loved this baby. I wouldn't lie in a court and say anything else."

When Tina had arrived, Jenna had taken the sleeping baby from the back car seat and asked Tina straight out about her part in Leeann's allegations against her. The misunderstanding had been cleared up quickly. Seemed Leeann hadn't even lodged a complaint. The story was just a manipulative ploy to gain her time and leverage.

Jenna stroked Meg's dimpled hand and reassured Tina again. "I didn't want to believe the worst. That's why we came here to speak with you about it."

Tina half smiled as she studied Meg. "I know she'll be happy with you. It's so important to have people who truly care."

Jenna thought of her own mother, how she and Amy

had had her for too brief a time. But she'd promised herself to hold onto the good memories and bury any regrets concerning her parents. Yes, her father had had his weaknesses; didn't everyone? But she knew he had loved her. She only wished he was alive to tell her now.

She brought herself back. "Does your family come from Sydney, Tina? Do your parents live close by?"

Tina gripped the bench slats. She kept her eyes on Meg. "I lost my parents when I was young. I grew up with a friend of my mother's. A lovely lady. She passed away last year."

Jenna's heart contracted. Meg, Tina as well as herself were all without their parents.

She put her hand over the younger woman's. "We'd love to have you come and stay with us."

Tina's attention kicked up, her eyes wide behind their lenses. "Really?"

"You can help me with all the things I need to learn about—" Jenna's voice broke and she tried again. "About being a mother."

She felt Amy's presence at that moment more powerfully than ever before. Twins shared a certain energy, were bound in ways other people couldn't comprehend. She and her sister had an even stronger bond now—one that Jenna would make her priority all the days of her life.

Gage joined them and Tina stood. "Perhaps I should put the baby in her room. She'll sleep for another hour yet." She blinked down at Jenna. "Unless you want to carry her up."

Jenna pushed to her feet and carefully handed Meg over. "I'll put her down later tonight." She'd dreamed so often of saying those words. Now it wasn't merely tonight, but every night from now on.

Tina took the baby and began to move off. But Gage put up a hand. "Just a minute."

With a pulse leaping in his firm shadowed jaw, he concentrated on Meg for the longest time. Then he lowered his head and gently kissed her brow. "God bless, little one."

As Tina left, Jenna moved forward and set her palms on Gage's shirt. She tugged his loosened tie. "Big day."

"One of the biggest." He brought her near, his linked hands resting low on her back. "You'll be okay now."

A wonderfully warm feeling seeped through her veins. She smiled. "We'll be more than okay."

He glanced behind at the last police car leaving. "They've searched the grounds and neighborhood for signs of dear Barry. No luck so far."

Jenna knew to her bones the authorities would catch him. It was only a matter of time. Putting those two on trial wouldn't bring her family back but at least justice would be served.

"You're staying here the night?"

She nodded. One last night. "Then I thought we could drive out to the country house, reintroduce Meg to that cubby house and slide. She might be a little young for them now, but it won't be long."

His eyes crinkled above a warm but somehow wistful smile, and his hands pressed on her back. "But you know this house will revert back to you, as will Darley Realty. Murderers don't get to benefit from their crimes."

She didn't want to talk about that now. She wanted to go inside and stand with Gage over Meg's cot, as they'd done that night in the country house. Lord, she couldn't believe this was over!

Shivering with the ecstasy of relief, she pushed up on tiptoe to kiss him, but he spoke before their lips could meet.

"Would you like me to look after the negotiations for the W.A. deal? There'll be a delay until the trial ends and Leeann is convicted."

Couldn't he read her eyes? She'd had a belly-full of Darley Realty's twists and turns for one day. Besides, the answer was obvious. "Why wouldn't you handle it?"

His jaw shifted and the brightness in his eyes seemed to fade. "Then I'll make some initial phone calls on your behalf and have Nick follow it up for you."

Time screeched to a halt then folded in on itself as a horrible dizzy feeling flashed through her. She tried to smile but her quivering mouth didn't want to play. "You're going somewhere?"

His lips thinned. "Dubai. Tomorrow. I may have enough time to salvage some aspect of the deal if I get over there now." His smile looked forced. "No rest for the wicked."

She searched his eyes. "I hear they're busy people."

"You heard right."

All Jenna's energy seemed to drain from her body. Earlier today she'd wanted to confess how she'd felt about him and their future. She'd all but convinced herself that he'd fallen in love with her, perhaps as deeply as she'd fallen back in love with him. Despite his philosophy that children needed a stable home life—a life Gage Cameron the loner tycoon couldn't provide—she'd begun to believe that he'd come around.

That he'd come home to stay.

But it seemed her prayers for one more miracle wouldn't be answered. Gage was pulling away. And there was nothing she could do about it. Nothing she *should* do about it…other than accept and be grateful for the time they'd shared. No regrets—even if it tore her heart out, she had to let him go and do it gracefully. It wasn't only her well-being at stake, but Meg's. That baby deserved her guardian's strength and total commitment, and a whole lot more besides.

Nevertheless, her fingers clung to his shirt as her eyes roamed his face, drinking in every beautifully chiseled feature, burning the image in her mind. Their short time together seemed to be running away from her like rainwater down a pipe.

"Thank you, Gage." Her throat was suddenly thick. "I'll never be able to repay you for all you've done."

His gaze settled on her lips while his heartbeat boomed against her palms. "The books are square. As of this minute, we're even."

Of course, that had been his motivation from the start. Not falling in love. Not staying forever, but rather settling a debt. *And* sampling previously forbidden fruits; to be fair, she'd wanted that too.

His pale eyes glistened in the afternoon sun. A moment longer and his Adam's apple bobbed as he swallowed.

"Jenna…I have to go."

She forced herself to step back and smile.

"I know."

I know.

Thirteen

"No messages, Mr. Cameron." The building's desk clerk glanced up from his reception monitor and smiled. "We'll see you back in Sydney soon, I hope."

Gage signed the departure printout with an impatient flourish. "Not for a while."

"Would you like us to make your penthouse available for lease to special clients? I had an inquiry today from New York."

He snapped the pen down. "Tell you what. It's for sale. See what you can get for it."

When he'd left Jenna yesterday, he'd driven straight here. He'd watched cable, downed two scotches, then fallen into bed…and slept not a wink. He'd tossed and turned every other minute of the long, lonely night. He kept feeling her beside him, seeing her lovely face, smelling the perfume of her hair. Every ounce of sanity was needed to persuade himself he'd done the right thing.

This morning he'd dressed feeling like a dog's breakfast—head pounding, tongue glued to the roof of his mouth. His muscles ached as if he'd come down with the flu. He never wanted to see those bedroom walls again.

The concierge strolled up and practically clicked his heels. "Your limousine will arrive shortly, Mr. Cameron. The driver's checked in and your jet is fueled and ready to depart for your journey to the Emirates."

"Very good." Gage popped a mint then dug into his pocket and slapped a large note into the man's hand.

The concierge beamed. "Hope to see you again soon, sir."

Gage scowled. He wished people would stop saying that.

He checked his watch then peered out the twenty-five-foot glass doors to the circular drive and its colorful hedges. He barely noticed the man and his young children trundling into the foyer. Neither did he listen to the conversation the man had with the clerk. He didn't want to even *look* at the man. Or the baby he held. Although he guessed it was a girl.

Roughly Meg's age.

The man spoke to him. "Excuse me."

Gage frowned. "For what?"

The man didn't seem to notice his foul mood. "I need a hand and the boys are too young to hold her. Do you mind? I'll only be a minute." He held out a baby dressed in pink.

Gage counted his heartbeats.

The last time he'd held a baby he'd gotten into a

whole pile of trouble—he'd come close to convincing himself that he might be able to cheat the past and pretend to be someone he wasn't.

The man smiled. "She's fast asleep. I'll only be a moment."

The willowy brunette behind the counter raised a hand. "I can hold her." She darted out.

Gage took the baby as the lady reached them.

He grinned. *Too late.*

While the father took care of his business and the disappointed brunette returned to her station, Gage told himself he wouldn't look down. He was a smart man and his smarts told him that to study this child up close could be dangerous.

Beside him, the man apologized: *Just a little longer.*

Gage nodded.

Outside, the stretch limo rolled up and the concierge waved to him.

Uncomfortable, Gage nodded again.

A film of cool sweat erupted around his suddenly too tight collar. He was leaving. For good. Surely one tiny peek couldn't hurt. His eye line trailed down and…Gage grinned.

Not as bad as he'd thought. Nowhere near the tug he'd expected. This baby was cute, but not as cute as Meg. This one's nose was bigger, and she didn't have the cleft in her chin that was more defined whenever Meg was asleep. Her hands were similar though. So tiny, with four dimples delineating each knuckle. Such little nails.

He raised her up then lowered her down.

Pretty much the same weight too.

He studied her face again. Rosebud mouth. Did they all suck like that in their sleep? He frowned. Maybe she was hungry. He wouldn't think about diapers. Diapers he didn't do. Diapers he left to Jenna.

The man was speaking to him. "She's a doll, isn't she?"

Gage nodded. "What's her name?"

"Sarah."

Sarah was a pretty name, but Meg…well, it sounded sweeter.

"Do you have a family?" the man asked.

Gage's insides clenched. The pain—the memories— were so powerful, he almost doubled over.

He handed Sarah back. "No, I don't."

He strode toward the limo, ears and eyes blocked to the man with his family. A young woman passed him on her way to the desk. Sarah's mother? She had that look about her. A look of happiness. Completeness.

What the hell was that like?

The uniformed driver tipped his cap and opened the door. "Shouldn't be any traffic holdups, Mr. Cameron."

Gage strode right past and down the street.

He couldn't get into that car. He needed fresh air and lots of it.

Grabbing his tie, he wound the knot down then ripped the crimson silk completely from his neck and stuffed it into his pocket.

What was wrong with him? He'd accomplished what he'd set out to do. *More.* His debt to Raphael was repaid. Jenna wouldn't have to worry about money for the rest of her life. She had her baby. She was *happy.* Most importantly, she wouldn't have him hanging around screwing with her emotions *or* her life.

He strode across the street, ignoring the pedestrian signal, the beeping horns, the annoyed glares.

God, he wanted her now. Almost enough to convince himself that he could *continue* to make her happy. But that pleasure had come at a cost. It was *pay up now* or *suffer later*. He'd lost count of the number of times they'd made love.

Now it was no longer safe.

He found himself at Darling Harbour. He should get out of here, as fast and far as those Learjet engines could carry him. But how could he sort out Dubai when his brain felt ready to explode?

At the end of a pier, he stopped to hold his head, clamping the ache, willing it to leave. But still the damning thoughts wheeled in.

All his life he'd wanted to escape…his Leave-it-to-Beaver peers in school, who didn't know how lucky they were…his poor wasted mother, who'd given up caring years before she'd died. Twelve years ago Gage had wanted to escape Jenna too, or rather had wanted her to be free of him. He'd found out yesterday that Jenna had paid dearly for having known him—a crippling bout of depression. Not so long ago, another woman hadn't gotten off that lightly.

Brittany Jackson had been one of his secretaries. On a business weekend away he'd let down his guard, broken his own rule and had slept with the besotted employee. He usually set limits on how long an affair would last. He liked to cut loose before strong attachments could be formed, but Brittany didn't make waves or demands. On top of that, she was discreet. He'd felt comfortable with her…until the day she'd told him she was pregnant.

Completely floored, he'd fallen back in his chair. She'd known his mind. He did *not* want children.

They'd always used precautions. What the hell had gone wrong? When she'd cried and run from his Melbourne home, he didn't follow. He had important business to conduct overseas. He'd planned to take her, but now he had to think.

Although they spoke on the phone, he'd stayed overseas for three weeks—quietly angry at her, but angrier at himself. Although he'd felt trapped, there'd been no doubt in his mind that he'd do the right thing—which also happened to be the worst thing. Money aside, what life would they have? He didn't love this woman. Brittany would grow to resent and perhaps even hate him for his ambivalence. But their child would suffer the most, growing up with a largely absent father and a needy, miserable mother. Hello, *twisted sense of self-worth.* Come on down, *a childhood of shame and rebellion.* Man, didn't that sound familiar.

When he'd finally returned to Sydney and marched into his office with a rock in his pocket and his proposal prepared, his P.A. walked straight in behind and shut the door. Bad news. Over the weekend, one of his secretaries, Brittany Jackson, had been killed in a car accident.

The horror had knocked him senseless. He'd put Brittany and his own child in their graves. If he'd taken her with him, they'd have been married and he'd have become a father. Instead, he'd let them down. Just as he'd let his mother and Jenna down when he'd left. Coming back here, all he'd wanted was to make amends. Atone for past mistakes. Find a little peace.

Gage fell onto his knees.

He didn't deserve happiness. Loner. Mystery man. Who was the enigma behind the mask? Gage knew the answer.

A man who wasn't sure whether to take a blessing and hold it with both hands, or walk away from disaster while there was still time.

Jenna stood outside the pool house. She was peering up at the jet inching its way across the dreary gray sky, taking its passengers to heaven knew where, for heaven knew how long.

The empty ache in her stomach flipped over and she screwed her eyes shut.

Stay strong. This is the last time you'll ever need to get over him. No more heartache, for you or for Meg.

After a long, settling breath, she turned the lock on the pool house door and took in a sweeping view of her childhood home. In the last ten years, she'd been all around the world. So where to now?

Not the country house that Gage had bought. She'd been happy about living there only when she'd fooled herself into thinking that Gage would live there, too. Now the prospect of settling in that house, filled with its bittersweet memories, was perhaps even worse than staying here.

She and Meg needed a fresh start. Somewhere where sad remembrances didn't haunt them and she could give her heart time to mend. Not that the wound would ever completely heal. From the moment she and Gage had locked gazes that summer long ago, she'd belonged to him. Although she would never again know the special magic of his embrace—of his kiss—she belonged to him still. Time and distance could never change that.

But she had what she'd prayed for—Meg safe and sound with her. That should be more than enough.

She pocketed the key.

It was better that Gage had gone. He'd always been a loner, a person who found reasons not to settle down. As much as it pained her, Gage had known best, and he was best shut out of their lives.

She rotated toward the house and collided with what felt like a solid brick wall. She gazed up into a pair of piercing gray eyes and gasped.

Her mind and heartbeat skidded to a stop. "What are *you* doing here?"

Gage's chest was pumping as if he'd run a marathon. "I needed to see you."

A lock of dark hair had fallen over his brow. Without a tie, his shirt was unbuttoned almost halfway, giving her a tantalizing peek at his chest. That scar on his mouth begged her fingertip to reach out and—

No!

She knocked those dangerous thoughts aside and straightened.

He'd said he needed to see her. Obviously nothing of an intimate nature; yesterday he'd made his final stand on that issue. So, his surprise visit must concern business—her father's company or the W.A. property.

She folded her arms. "I know what I said yesterday, but I'm more than capable of taking care of Darley Realty's concerns from here on." She offered a tight smile. "Thanks again."

She began to circumnavigate the pool on her way to the house.

"This doesn't concern Darley Realty."

Thinking of the jet that had flown overhead, she looked back. "Why aren't you on your way to Dubai? Problems over there were supposed to be urgent."

He joined her. "They are urgent. But nothing compared to this."

A flash of panic raced up her spine. But she knew this couldn't be about Meg; everything was squared away there. She also knew that saying goodbye to Gage yesterday had been painful enough. If she had to go through it again, better to have it over with quickly, like the drop of a guillotine blade.

She set her hands on her hips. "What's this about, Gage?" *Spit it out.*

He took her hands from her hips and held them together in his. "I don't want this to end. What we have is too good to throw away."

Even as the physical contact released within her a surge of desperate longing, she set her jaw. Yesterday, he'd vanished from her life—*again.* From the start, he'd been upfront and she would deal with that…somehow. But now he'd returned, wanting her back in his bed?

It didn't work that way.

"You're suggesting our mock marriage continue?"

"Yes." He frowned and shook his head. "I mean, no."

Her smile was as sad as it was dry. "I know what you mean. You want to be able to fly into Sydney and see that my bedroom door is always open."

"It's far more complicated than that."

She'd never felt more alive—more like a woman—than when she'd been with him. She hadn't thought it possible to feel so whole and new. But having her deepest intimate fantasies come true had also made clear what she'd known all along.

"It's not so complicated, Gage. You told me, remember? You don't grow roots." He didn't do *family.*

"What we shared was good, but it was temporary."
Now it was over.

"I want us to be more than temporary."

She almost laughed. "You'd like to block off another few weeks in your calendar?"

She flinched at her own shrewish tone, but her sarcasm covered red, raw pain. He was playing with her heart. Damn it, she was worth more than that.

Her eye line dropped. Her fingers were clutching his as though her life depended on it.

Mortified, she stepped back. "You should go."

He planted his feet shoulder-width apart. "I can't."

"Then I will." She walked away, around the pool's edge to avoid a puddle from the morning's rain.

He called after her. "I want to make you happy—make *us* happy."

She said casually, over her shoulder. "And you'll accomplish that how?"

"We should stay married. Really married."

That jolted her back. But of course that scenario would be part of his *what we have is too good to throw away* plan. What did "real" marriage mean to a man like Gage? Commitment or, more likely, convenience? Besides, staying married wouldn't fix things. She was a mother now, with a mother's concerns.

When she turned to face him, the pool's blue width stretched between them. "You said it at the start… marriage isn't the issue. I have a child to consider. I won't put my passions before Meg's well-being. If she comes to look upon you as a father—a father who is constantly saying goodbye—that will leave scars. If I let that happen, I'm no less selfish than Leeann."

Girls needed to depend on their fathers. She knew that better than anyone.

"Jenna, I need to tell you…I've done things in my past I'm not proud of."

Her heart tugged at the open expression on his face, of whatever secrets he seemed willing to reveal. But there was no need.

"We've all done things we regret." Like leaving her family in a huff and letting pride keep her away far too long. "But there's no need to feel guilty about what's happened these past weeks. You did more than you'd set out to do. I'm grateful for everything. But don't mess it up. It's time to move on."

His voice lowered. "I want us to be a family. A whole family."

Her heart thudded in her chest. It sounded as if he'd really missed them. Heck, maybe today he truly *did* want that family. But what about the sense of desolation she'd suffered when he'd walked away from her yesterday? Did he expect her to fall at his feet without considering the real possibility of a third goodbye?

Her stomach muscles tightened.

Sorry, she just couldn't.

She turned on her heel to leave.

"Jenna, I love you."

Those words stole her breath away. Despite it all, she ached to say them, too. She'd whispered them so often in her mind. But that kind of confession wouldn't change things, other than to leave her more vulnerable.

"If you want me to give up my work," he continued. "I will. I don't care about Dubai. I don't care about money."

Her heart aching, she turned to face him. "It's not

making money that you'd miss. It'd be the loss of doing it so well. It's who you are, Gage. If you gave it all up, you'd be itching to find yourself again, by jumping on a jet, making another million, just wanting to escape."

If she said yes to him now and he left her a third time…

Tears blurred her sight.

Damn it, she'd sworn he'd never hurt her again.

His voice reached her over the water. "It wouldn't be like that."

Her heart tore down the middle. "You of all people can't give me that promise."

She only wished he *could* convince her.

As she started to turn from him, her foot slipped on the wet tiles.

One second she was falling face-first toward the water, the next she belly flopped *hard* into the deep end. Jenna opened her mouth to cry out at the same time she landed in the water. Pain radiated through her as she flailed, swallowed water and began to sink.

Only seconds later, she was half aware of being dragged up and breaking the water's surface. She opened her eyes. Gage's strong arms were hoisting her out onto the pool's edge. While she spluttered and coughed, he pulled himself out. Water coursing down his worried face, he knelt and carefully held her in his lap. The pain throbbed worse; she cringed and shut her eyes.

He stood up and swept her into his arms. "I'm getting you to a doctor."

As Gage strode with her toward the house, she gingerly moved her arms and legs. She hadn't hit the side. Nothing felt broken.

When they reached the back patio, she'd stopped coughing and her head wasn't quite so foggy.

"I'm all right," Jenna murmured. "You can put me down."

"I told you, I'm taking you to a doctor."

He gazed down at her, his eyes fiery, his hair swept back, his hard body not quite trembling as he held her. And then she realized.

Warmth spread through her chest and she smiled. "You're all wet."

He didn't look impressed. "So it seems."

"I thought you'd rather eat razor blades than try to swim."

He'd acted without thinking and had faced his greatest fear when he thought she was in trouble. He said he wanted her to trust him…said he would give up his Fortune 500 lifestyle….

Her mind was still reeling when, sopping wet and cold, he brought his mouth to hers, kissing her with all the fire and honesty she'd lain awake and dreamt of last night. Intense, passionate. Overwhelming and fulfilling.

Panicking, she broke the kiss. "Your cell phone! It'll be ruined, and it has all that footage of Leeann and Barry and—"

He set her feet gently on the ground. "The police already have a copy of the incident and the phone."

He gathered her close. The kiss this time was slow and deep.

She came up for air, dreamy, the fall into the pool almost forgotten, but she needed to ask, "I thought you were certain that you wanted the plane not the anchor."

His brows lifted. "My pen?" She nodded. "My Montblanc is sitting on the bottom of Darling Harbour, or, perhaps, in the belly of some fish."

"Did you drop it?"

"No. I tossed it as far as I could. It flew for a while then sank, a little like you a minute ago." He grinned and held her closer. "You and Meg are what's real to me, nothing else. You're who I am, what I need. Not big contracts signed with gold pens. Not Maseratis or Learjets. I'm nothing without your love. All these years, I was nothing without you."

Jenna gazed up into those incredible eyes, wanting, needing to believe. Her concentration slipped when she heard a distant voice.

"What's going on here?" Tina called out from the far end of the patio. "Do you two often go swimming fully dressed?"

In her nanny's arms, Meg cooed and wriggled.

"Jenna slipped and fell into the pool," Gage explained.

Without another word, Tina disappeared inside. She returned with Meg in one arm and towels under the other. Jenna and Gage gratefully accepted a towel each while Tina asked if Jenna was all right and Jenna assured everyone she really was fine.

After Gage had wiped himself down, he dropped his wet towel, took the last dry one from Tina and held out his arms.

"May I?" He took the baby, sitting her in the towel and gazed down lovingly. "I'm going to be here for you. First words, first steps, first day of school. I'm looking forward to every moment."

Eyes bright and blue, Meg laughed and tried to clap.

Tina laughed too. "Looks like she missed her dad."

Jenna held her breath.

But Gage only smiled. "And I missed her, so much you wouldn't believe."

Tears prickled Jenna's eyes. Could Gage—a professed loner—be a stable father for her baby? Would Amy and Brad have wanted that? More importantly, was that what Meg needed?

He brought Jenna close and brushed his lips against her temple. "I want to be Meg's dad. And I want to be your husband, for real, Jenna. Forever. We deserve this chance. We all deserve some happiness."

Jenna pressed her lips together. They really did deserve happiness, didn't they? Little Meg more than anyone. Perhaps it wasn't wrong to trust one more time, to put her faith in her love and in his.

His tone deepened. "Tell me you love me. Seems I've waited my whole life to hear it."

When, perched between them, Meg placed one hand on his chest and one hand on hers, Jenna felt herself being swept away on the first leg of a beautiful journey. With a smile, she released the last of her fears. "I love you. I've never stopped loving you. I never will."

His eyes glistened as they searched hers. "Then I'm one very happy man."

When their mouths joined above their baby's head, Jenna felt so many powerful forces swirling around them—forming, then sparking and finally melding together to shine more brightly than ever before.

She felt it to her soul.

This union was indeed a match made in heaven. A wonderful heaven on earth.

Epilogue

Four years later

At the light tap on the door, Jenna set down her nail file and pushed up higher on her family-sized hospital bed. A little weary, but so very happy, she beamed when her husband and excited little girl entered her private maternity suite.

Meg, with her blond pigtails, bounced onto the mattress and crawled over to lie beside her mother. She pressed a big wet kiss on Jenna's cheek.

"I missed you, Mummy."

Gage leant over Meg to give his wife his own kiss, the kind of heart-warming, tender caress that would live on in her memory forever. He smiled into her eyes. "You've never looked more beautiful."

She might have laughed. After giving birth, minus

makeup? But the sincerity shining from his eyes sent her fingers curving around his jaw. How she loved this man—so much it sometimes hurt.

Holding her gaze with his, he pressed her palm to his lips then straightened. "These are for you."

From behind his back, he whipped out a bouquet of wildflowers.

Vibrant yellows, soft pinks, striking reds...

"They're beautiful!" Jenna reached for the call button. "I'll have a nurse bring a vase."

His fingers folded over hers. "The nurses have their hands full right now."

"Daddy said there'd be a big surprise when we got here." Meg looked up at her mother and whispered, "I know what the surprise is."

Gage tickled his daughter's ribs. "I'll bet you don't."

On cue, a pair of nurses strolled in, each carrying a cherished bundle.

Meg's hands flew to her mouth at the same time Gage set down the flowers and put out his arms.

His eyes were sparkling—with happiness, wonder, heartfelt thanks—the same gamut of emotions that ignited and twirled through Jenna too. How many moments were there as precious as this? Today must be the happiest of her life.

Gage carefully took the nearest baby. "Which one's this?" He shifted the blanket a smidgeon to look at the face. "Ah, Noah." His smile grew. "What a handsome boy."

The second nurse laid the other twin in Jenna's arms. Jenna inspected the baby's features and grinned. And Isobelle was a gorgeous girl.

Meg's eyebrows sloped, pleading, "Can I hold one?"

"Your little sister or your brother?" Gage asked, indicating with a nudge of his chin that Meg should wriggle back against the pillows.

"Um…that one," she answered, pointing to the bundle in Gage's arms.

Positioned and ready, Meg's eyes widened with amazement as Gage laid a soundly sleeping Noah in her arms. "I can't believe I get *two* babies." When Noah yawned, Meg's sigh went on forever. "I love him," she murmured adoringly. Then she frowned. "But he needs a iron. He's got some wrinkles."

Gage laughed. "That's because he's brand new. He'll fill out soon enough." He tugged one of Meg's pigtail. "You certainly did. Look at you!"

A short time ago Meg had been a baby, too. Both Jenna and Gage had loved and nurtured her; she'd been their whole world. Meg was so comfortable with herself—so sweet yet confident—Jenna knew they'd done a fine job so far.

Jenna tilted closer to Meg. "Why don't you kiss Noah's brow? He'd like that."

Meg pressed her lips to the baby's head. Her small fingers patted the baby blanket as she would her favorite swaddled doll. She couldn't take her eyes off him.

"Can we take them home now?"

Gage stroked Meg's crown. "Not yet, honey. A few more days."

Both babies were a good weight, and there'd been no complications. But, even with Tina's assistance, Jenna needed to regain her strength before tackling the rewarding yet tiring task of caring for newborn twins.

"Are you sure you'll be okay with Meg at home by yourself?" she asked.

Gage pretended to scoff. "We'll have fun."

Meg gave a very grown-up nod. "And the new lady's there to do all the dishes and stuff."

Gage's jaw shifted. "Hey, I can do dishes."

Meg rolled her eyes as if to say, *Well, he tries.*

Gage rounded the bed and sat beside Jenna. "Don't worry about us. Concentrate on building up your strength." His mouth kicked into a playful smile, but his eyes were bright with a deeper emotion. "I'm not surprised you make beautiful babies."

Her gaze ran over the lips she would never grow tired of kissing each morning and every night. "*We* make beautiful babies."

He curled a knuckle around his baby daughter's cheek. "I felt complete before," he murmured, "but *this…*" His shoulders went back. "We'll just have to have more."

Jenna coughed out a laugh. "Can I have a few weeks?"

But of course she wanted more children as much as he did. She'd taken three years to get pregnant. Perhaps the delay was partly due to stress over the trial. Now that her stepmother and Barry Whitmore were serving hard time, Jenna would be happy never to hear their names again.

Gage had been at her side the entire time, except for three days away to save the Dubai deal, which Jenna had insisted on. Then he'd handed over most of his business responsibilities to Nick, who had since married Summer. In his spare time, Gage helped his wife with her directorship of Darley Realty and restored classic cars. His latest work—an Aston Martin DB4 convertible—had sold for an obscene amount at auction.

In four years they'd become so close. He'd told her about that poor woman, Brittany—on top of everything else, no wonder Gage had been terrified to commit. And now little Meg was in Prep—the year of formal schooling before the Big Grade One. She was so bright; Jenna had wondered whether her daughter would somehow work out that her mummy was having twins. Seeing Meg's face now, keeping the surprise had been well worth it.

Gage toyed with Isobelle's tiny hand. "Did you know that 22 percent of twins are left-handed as opposed to 10 percent of nontwins?"

Jenna nodded. "I think you mentioned it." At least a dozen times since they'd learned this would be a multiple birth.

"And the word *twin,*" he went on, "comes from the Greek word *twine,* which means two together."

"Like a tree," Meg offered.

"Sure," he said. "Branches can twine."

"And spread out." Meg spoke to Jenna. "Miss Samuels told us today at school."

Gage smiled mysteriously. "We should show Mummy the special tree you and Miss Samuels made today."

Meg's face lit up. "Can you get it, Daddy?"

Gage retrieved a folded piece of paper from Meg's sequined handbag. He opened it then held the paper up so proudly, it might have been the deeds to a palace. "Meg drew our family tree."

Meg chimed in. "See. There's me and Noah…or Iz-zybelle. I thought there was one." She tilted her head at the paper. "Here's you and Daddy. Daddy's got a crown coz he comes from kings. And there's my other mummy and dad."

The twist of pain in Jenna's chest was quickly replaced by the warmth of love. She could barely see through her welling tears. Standing to either side of the stick figures that represented herself and Gage were another couple who wore bright yellow halos.

"They're our garjon angels," Meg said earnestly. "Noah and Izzy's angels now, too." She turned her big blue eyes up at Jenna. "If you're not too tired, Mummy, I want to take a photo of us here for Show and Tell."

Smiling, Jenna cleared the thickness from her throat. "I'm not too tired, sweetheart."

Gage pretimed the camera then set it on the portable meal table at the end of the bed. Sitting beside Meg, he laid his arm along the pillows at their backs and brought his family near.

He winked at Jenna, kissed Meg's crown then smiled into the lens. "Everyone say, *chocolate fudge sundae!*"

The flash went off, but Jenna's smile didn't fade. She wanted this moment to last and last.

Gage nudged her. "Hey, you're off with the fairies. Penny for your thoughts."

She was thinking she'd been given the most priceless gifts in the world—her husband, her family and a loving, stable home where each of them would always belong.

"I was thinking that no one could be happier than I am right now," she admitted.

Gage leant close, and his adoring smile grazed her lips. "No one except me."

* * * * *

Here is a sneak preview of
A STONE CREEK CHRISTMAS,
the latest in Linda Lael Miller's acclaimed
McKETTRICK *series.*

A lonely horse brought vet Olivia O'Ballivan to
Tanner Quinn's farm, but it's the rancher's love
that might cause her to stay.

A STONE CREEK CHRISTMAS
Available December 2008
from Silhouette Special Edition

Tanner heard the rig roll in around sunset. Smiling, he wandered to the window. Watched as Olivia O'Ballivan climbed out of her Suburban, flung one defiant glance toward the house and started for the barn, the golden retriever trotting along behind her.

Taking his coat and hat down from the peg next to the back door, he put them on and went outside. He was used to being alone, even liked it, but keeping company with Doc O'Ballivan, bristly though she sometimes was, would provide a welcome diversion.

He gave her time to reach the horse Butterpie's stall, then walked into the barn.

The golden retriever came to greet him, all wagging tail and melting brown eyes, and he bent to stroke her soft, sturdy back. "Hey, there, dog," he said.

Sure enough, Olivia was in the stall, brushing But-

terpie down and talking to her in a soft, soothing voice
that touched something private inside Tanner and made
him want to turn on one heel and beat it back to the
house.

He'd be damned if he'd do it, though.

This was *his* ranch, *his* barn. Well-intentioned as
she was, *Olivia* was the trespasser here, not him.

"She's still very upset," Olivia told him, without
turning to look at him or slowing down with the brush.

Shiloh, always an easy horse to get along with, stood
contentedly in his own stall, munching away on the
feed Tanner had given him earlier. Butterpie, he noted,
hadn't touched her supper as far as he could tell.

"Do you know anything at all about horses, Mr.
Quinn?" Olivia asked.

He leaned against the stall door, the way he had the
day before, and grinned. He'd practically been raised
on horseback; he and Tessa had grown up on their
grandmother's farm in the Texas hill country, after their
folks divorced and went their separate ways, both of
them too busy to bother with a couple of kids. "A few
things," he said. "And I mean to call you Olivia, so you
might as well return the favor and address me by my
first name."

He watched as she took that in, dealt with it, decided
on an approach. He'd have to wait and see what that
turned out to be, but he didn't mind. It was a pleasure
just watching Olivia O'Ballivan grooming a horse.

"All right, *Tanner*," she said. "This barn is a disgrace.
When are you going to have the roof fixed? If it snows
again, the hay will get wet and probably mold..."

He chuckled, shifted a little. He'd have a crew out
there the following Monday morning to replace the

roof and shore up the walls—he'd made the arrangements over a week before—but he felt no particular compunction to explain that. He was enjoying her ire too much; it made her color rise and her hair fly when she turned her head, and the faster breathing made her perfect breasts go up and down in an enticing rhythm. "What makes you so sure I'm a greenhorn?" he asked mildly, still leaning on the gate.

At last she looked straight at him, but she didn't move from Butterpie's side. "Your hat, your boots— that fancy red truck you drive. I'll bet it's customized."

Tanner grinned. Adjusted his hat. "Are you telling me real cowboys don't drive red trucks?"

"There are lots of trucks around here," she said. "Some of them are red, and some of them are new. And *all* of them are splattered with mud or manure or both."

"Maybe I ought to put in a car wash, then," he teased. "Sounds like there's a market for one. Might be a good investment."

She softened, though not significantly, and spared him a cautious half smile, full of questions she probably wouldn't ask. "There's a good car wash in Indian Rock," she informed him. "People go there. It's only forty miles."

"Oh," he said with just a hint of mockery. "*Only* forty miles. Well, then. Guess I'd better dirty up my truck if I want to be taken seriously in these here parts. Scuff up my boots a bit, too, and maybe stomp on my hat a couple of times."

Her cheeks went a fetching shade of pink. "You are twisting what I said," she told him, brushing Butterpie again, her touch gentle but sure. "I meant…"

Tanner envied that little horse. Wished he had a furry hide, so he'd need brushing, too.

"You *meant* that I'm not a real cowboy," he said. "And you could be right. I've spent a lot of time on construction sites over the last few years, or in meetings where a hat and boots wouldn't be appropriate. Instead of digging out my old gear, once I decided to take this job, I just bought new."

"I bet you don't even *have* any old gear," she challenged, but she was smiling, albeit cautiously, as though she might withdraw into a disapproving frown at any second.

He took off his hat, extended it to her. "Here," he teased. "Rub that around in the muck until it suits you."

She laughed, and the sound—well, it caused a powerful and wholly unexpected shift inside him. Scared the hell out of him and, paradoxically, made him yearn to hear it again.

* * * * *

*Discover how this rugged rancher's wanderlust
is tamed in time for a merry Christmas, in
A STONE CREEK CHRISTMAS.
In stores December 2008.*

Silhouette®

SPECIAL EDITION™

FROM *NEW YORK TIMES* BESTSELLING AUTHOR

LINDA LAEL MILLER

A STONE CREEK CHRISTMAS

Veterinarian Olivia O'Ballivan finds the animals in Stone Creek playing Cupid between her and Tanner Quinn. Even Tanner's daughter, Sophie, is eager to play matchmaker. With everyone conspiring against them and the holiday season fast approaching, Tanner and Olivia may just get everything they want for Christmas after all!

Available December 2008
wherever books are sold.

SPECIAL EDITION™

MISTLETOE AND MIRACLES

by *USA TODAY* bestselling author
MARIE FERRARELLA

Child psychologist Trent Marlowe couldn't believe his eyes when Laurel Greer, the woman he'd loved and lost, came to him for help. Now a widow, with a troubled boy who wouldn't speak, Laurel needed a miracle from Trent…and a brief detour under the mistletoe wouldn't hurt, either.

Available in December wherever books are sold.

THE ITALIAN'S BRIDE

Commanded—to be his wife!

Used to the finest food, clothes and women,
these immensely powerful, incredibly
good-looking and undeniably charismatic
men have only one last need: a wife!

They've chosen their bride-to-be and they'll
have her—willing or not!

Enjoy all our fantastic stories in December:

THE ITALIAN BILLIONAIRE'S SECRET LOVE-CHILD
by CATHY WILLIAMS (Book #33)

SICILIAN MILLIONAIRE, BOUGHT BRIDE
by CATHERINE SPENCER (Book #34)

BEDDED AND WEDDED FOR REVENGE
by MELANIE MILBURNE (Book #35)

THE ITALIAN'S UNWILLING WIFE
by KATHRYN ROSS (Book #36)

REQUEST YOUR FREE BOOKS!

2 FREE NOVELS PLUS 2 FREE GIFTS!

Silhouette®

Desire®

Passionate, Powerful, Provocative!

YES! Please send me 2 FREE Silhouette Desire® novels and my 2 FREE gifts (gifts are worth about $10). After receiving them, if I don't wish to receive any more books, I can return the shipping statement marked "cancel". If I don't cancel, I will receive 6 brand-new novels every month and be billed just $4.05 per book in the U.S. or $4.74 per book in Canada, plus 25¢ shipping and handling per book and applicable taxes, if any*. That's a savings of almost 15% off the cover price! I understand that accepting the 2 free books and gifts places me under no obligation to buy anything. I can always return a shipment and cancel at any time. Even if I never buy another book, the two free books and gifts are mine to keep forever. 225 SDN ERVX 326 SDN ERVM

Name _____ (PLEASE PRINT)

Address _____ Apt. #

City _____ State/Prov. _____ Zip/Postal Code

Signature (if under 18, a parent or guardian must sign)

Mail to the **Silhouette Reader Service:**
IN U.S.A.: P.O. Box 1867, Buffalo, NY 14240-1867
IN CANADA: P.O. Box 609, Fort Erie, Ontario L2A 5X3

Not valid to current subscribers of Silhouette Desire books.

Want to try two free books from another line?
Call 1-800-873-8635 or visit www.morefreebooks.com.

* Terms and prices subject to change without notice. N.Y. residents add applicable sales tax. Canadian residents will be charged applicable provincial taxes and GST. Offer not valid in Quebec. This offer is limited to one order per household. All orders subject to approval. Credit or debit balances in a customer's account(s) may be offset by any other outstanding balance owed by or to the customer. Please allow 4 to 6 weeks for delivery. Offer available while quantities last.

Your Privacy: Silhouette Books is committed to protecting your privacy. Our Privacy Policy is available online at www.eHarlequin.com or upon request from the Reader Service. From time to time we make our lists of customers available to reputable third parties who may have a product or service of interest to you. If you would prefer we not share your name and address, please check here. ☐

SDES08R

Santa's finally figured out
what women want—hot guys!
And these three lucky ladies unwrap
three of the hottest men around.
Don't miss Harlequin Blaze's new
Christmas anthology, guaranteed
to live up to its title!

HEATING UP
THE HOLIDAYS

A Hunky Holiday Collection

Available in December
wherever books are sold.

nocturne™

New York Times bestselling author

MERLINE LOVELACE

LORI DEVOTI

HOLIDAY WITH A VAMPIRE II

**CELEBRATE THE HOLIDAYS WITH TWO
BREATHTAKING STORIES FROM
NEW YORK TIMES BESTSELLING AUTHOR
MERLINE LOVELACE AND LORI DEVOTI.**

Two vampires, each wary of human relationships,
are put to the test when holiday encounters blur
the boundaries of passion and hunger.

Available December wherever books are sold.

SN61801